## "I can'... se...

"Can't you?" Oliver's voice was gently mocking. "Come on, Fliss. Who do you think you're fooling? Me? Or yourself?"

"How dare you!"

"How dare I what? Remind you that you're not as composed as you'd like to think? You may look as if you've got a mouthful of ice cubes, but we both know better. You're such a delicious mix of virgin and wanton!"

*ANNE MATHER* began writing when she was a child, progressing through torrid teenage romances to the kind of adult romances she likes to read. She's married, with two children, and she lives in the north of England. After writing, she enjoys reading, driving and traveling to different places to find settings for new novels. She considers herself very lucky to do something that she not only enjoys, but also gets paid for.

## Books by Anne Mather

Don't miss any of our special offers. Write to us at the following address for information on our newest releases.

Harlequin Reader Service
U.S.: 3010 Walden Ave., P.O. Box 1325, Buffalo, NY 14269
Canadian: P.O. Box 609, Fort Erie, Ont. L2A 5X3

# Anne Mather

## Raw Silk

**Harlequin Books**

TORONTO • NEW YORK • LONDON
AMSTERDAM • PARIS • SYDNEY • HAMBURG
STOCKHOLM • ATHENS • TOKYO • MILAN
MADRID • WARSAW • BUDAPEST • AUCKLAND

ISBN 0-373-11731-0

RAW SILK

Copyright © 1994 by Anne Mather.

First North American Publication 1995.

**Printed in U.S.A.**

# CHAPTER ONE

THE sunset was spectacular, spilling its crimson light over clouds that already had a tinge of purple about them. It wasn't gentle, and it wasn't peaceful, but its sombre, brooding presence mirrored Oliver's mood.

He stood at the apartment window, long legs braced, shoulders set, hands thrust deep into his trouser pockets, gazing out at the view that encompassed half the Tsim Sha Tsui peninsula. It should have soothed him, but it didn't. By anyone's reckoning it was impressive, with the hillside falling away to give an uninterrupted view of the harbour. And there was the Hong Kong skyline rising across the water, acres of solid real estate in concrete, steel and glass. But Oliver was not impressed; he scarcely even saw it.

'But, darling, you have to come with me!'

Behind him, Rose Chen's voice persisted in its persuasive refrain. For over an hour the delicate Chinese girl had been trying to convince him that she couldn't go to England without him, and for equally that long Oliver had been insisting that she must.

'Why?' he asked again, for at least the tenth time. 'You're not a child, Rose. You don't need me to hold your hand.'

'Oh, but I do!' With a little cry, Rose Chen abandoned the provocative position she had been sustaining on the wide, oriental-quilted bed, and came to drape herself about him. With the sole of one foot sensuously caressing his calf, and her arms wound around his waist, her soft cheek pressed against his spine, she repeated her assertion. 'Darling, I've never been to London. You

5

have. I need you to come with me. They're going to hate me, aren't they? I need your support.'

Oliver withstood her concerted attempts to arouse him with admirable restraint. It would be so easy to succumb to her allure, so easy to relax and give in to everything she asked of him. Rose Chen was nothing if not dedicated in everything she did, and the sinuous little body, clad only in a silk robe, arched against his back, was undeniably tempting. Even though he was dressed, he could feel her pointed little breasts through the thin silk of his shirt.

But unfortunately for Rose Chen Oliver had a strength of will that equalled her own. And he also knew that the Chinese girl wasn't half as helpless as she liked him to think. Rose Chen could be quite ruthless when it came to business, and he had no doubt at all that she could handle her London relations without any assistance from him.

And that reminded him that he had to stop thinking of her as being wholly Chinese. She wasn't. She was half English. Amazingly, she had been James Hastings' daughter. Not his mistress, as his own government had believed, but the illegitimate offspring of a liaison Hastings had had before Oliver had thought of crawling through the stinking jungles of South-east Asia. Which had altered the situation considerably...

'You'll make it,' he assured her now, removing the slim hand which had been attempting to unzip his fly, aware as he did so of the half-hearted arousal she had achieved. Obviously, his body was not as easy to control as his mind, which was some justification for the frustrated cry his action solicited.

'Don't you want me?' she exclaimed, her oval eyes narrowed and appealing, and Oliver wondered, somewhat ruefully, why he'd let it get this far.

But when he'd been recruited by a United States government agency to carry out a surveillance operation on James Hastings he had found a small irony in attracting and seducing the woman he had believed to be the Englishman's mistress.

Rose Chen had worked with James Hastings. She knew him well. When he had visited the Colony, he had stayed in the same apartment building she did. Not in the same apartment, as Oliver now knew, but that was splitting hairs. The fact remained that James Hastings had treated her rather well, and Rose Chen lived in vastly superior surroundings to those her salary at the import and export company Hastings had run would warrant.

Besides, it had seemed such a satisfactory solution to the problem of getting close enough to James Hastings to find out his comings and goings. No one, least of all the arrogant Englishman, had suspected Oliver of being anything more than the war-weary veteran he appeared. Hong Kong was full of drop-outs from one part of the world or another, and it was true that when Oliver had arrived in the territories he had been nothing more nor less than any of his fellow exiles.

In the beginning he hadn't much cared about anything or anybody. He was still escaping the horrors of a war that had gone so dreadfully wrong. He didn't care about the future. He tried not to think about the past. He lived his life from day to day, seeking oblivion with any kind of anaesthetic available.

Of course, his family had expected him to return to the United States when his term of duty was over, but Oliver hadn't done that. Not then. He couldn't bear the thought of returning home to Maple Falls, where life was so clean and simple. His mind was still trapped in the jungle, with the poor, pathetic victims of someone else's conflict.

Ironically enough, it was the army that had eventually rescued him, and restored his self-respect. Or his retired commanding officer, to be precise. Colonel Archibald Lightfoot had swept him off the streets—where he had been living since his severance pay ran out—and installed him in a rehabilitation clinic. And by the time his system had been laundered his mind was clear as well. That was when he had returned to the States—but only for a visit. The colonel had persuaded him he could be some use to him in the territories, and instead of becoming the youngest district attorney in his home state of Virginia he had returned to Hong Kong.

Naturally, his family had been disappointed. His father, once an attorney himself, but now a Supreme Court judge, had expected his eldest son to follow in his footsteps. His younger brothers and sisters were all employed in one aspect of the law or another, all safely married and settled, and a credit to the family. Only Oliver had refused to conform; only Oliver had let them down: first, by volunteering for Vietnam, and then by returning to live in South-east Asia.

These days his family knew better than to criticise his motives. His work for the Hong Kong government, and for the United States agency involved in the control of narcotic substances, had enabled him to amass a fairly substantial bank account, and although his job required him to live in fairly modest surroundings he owned an apartment in Kowloon just as comfortable as Rose Chen's. He was a valued member of Colonel Lightfoot's staff, and when he eventually chose to return to the United States he had the necessary contacts to find suitable employment there.

Of course, Rose Chen knew nothing of his involvement with the agency. So far as she was concerned, Oliver lived by his wits, making enough money from so-called 'deals' the agency sent his way to enable him to support the lifestyle he maintained. The fact that he seldom discussed his own affairs had convinced her that what he was doing wasn't exactly legal, a belief he nurtured on every possible occasion. He had wanted Rose,

nd James Hastings, to think he was corruptible. It suited
is purposes very well.

Not that Oliver was thinking of this now as he watched
he glittering display of neon that was emerging as the
ights were turned on in the tall buildings lower down
he hillside and across the water. Darkness gave the city
a different kind of energy, an energy that masked the
bject poverty found on the streets below.

'I'm not coming to London,' he stated flatly, moving
ut of her embrace. 'I'll take you to the airport, but
hat's as far as I go.'

Rose Chen's rose-tinted lips took on a sulky curve.
Suntong will take me to the airport,' she declared
hortly, and Oliver inclined his dark head.

'Of course he will,' he agreed, acknowledging her new
uthority over her father's massively fat chauffeur.
So...' He spread his hands. 'When are you planning
n leaving?'

'Soon.'

Rose Chen regarded him with dark hostile eyes. The
vidence of her frustration was there in every line of her
lim, provocative body. Rose Chen generally got what
he wanted, and right now she wanted him. Wanted him
o badly, in fact, that she had even risked the wrath of
er employer.

No, not her employer, Oliver reminded himself yet
gain. Her *father*! The father she hadn't known she'd
ad until his death in England had necessitated the news
o be conveyed to her. It had been there, in his will, all
long. As well as the son, who had expected to inherit
is father's company, James Hastings had at last ac-
nowledged the existence of his daughter. Rose Chen
as to share everything he had left, including half his
ssets in London.

'Please, Lee,' she begged now, and Oliver realised that,
hile he had been considering what this new devel-
pment might mean to his investigation, Rose Chen's

face had undergone another change of expression. 'Please,' she said again, 'change your mind. This is all so new to me. Jay-Jay never even hinted that he might be—that he was my——' She broke off and wrung her slender hands together. 'You can't know what this means to me. If only I'd known...'

Oliver's sympathies were stirred. He knew, better than anyone, how persuasive Rose Chen could be if she set her mind to it. Images of her naked body entwined with his were all too vivid a memory when she looked at him that way, and in the pearly evening twilight her sexuality was almost irresistible.

'And what am I supposed to do while you deal with these new relatives of yours?' he enquired softly, as the obvious reaction Colonel Lightfoot would have to her sudden change of status forced him to reconsider. It was almost certain that the colonel would consider the opportunity for a closer look at the London end of Hastings' operation too important to miss, and, while Oliver had no real desire to accompany her, the prospect of an expenses-paid trip to England was not unappealing.

Rose Chen's oval eyes widened. 'You'll come?' She caught her breath and started towards him. 'Oh, Lee——'

'I didn't say that,' he stalled her, holding up a warning hand. 'I was just curious to know how you would introduce me. I don't think your brother will welcome an intruder.'

'You mean *another* intruder,' said Rose Chen shrewdly, and then snapped her fingers. 'What do I care what—Robert,' she said the name experimentally, 'thinks? He hasn't even responded to the fax I sent him when I was first informed of Jay-Jay's death. Before I even knew Jay-Jay was my father.' Her lips twisted. 'It was a shock even then.'

Oliver shrugged. 'I doubt it's been easy for Robert either,' he remarked drily, but Rose Chen's expression showed no compassion.

'No,' she answered, her tone mirroring little concern for her half-brother's feelings. She looked pensive for a moment, and then, as if dismissing what she had been thinking, she looked at him again. 'So—will you come with me? It would mean so much to me if you would. You're the only person I care two figs about.'

Oliver's mouth thinned. 'What about your mother?'

'Her?' Rose Chen looked contemptuous. 'She's never cared about me, so why should I care about her? Besides, she doesn't approve of me. She never wanted me to work for Jay-Jay in the first place. Now, I know why.'

Oliver frowned. 'Does she know about——?' He paused and arched his brows with obvious intent. 'Have you seen her since the lawyer contacted you?'

'No.' Rose Chen pushed her hands inside the wide sleeves of her robe and hugged them to her. 'It's nothing to do with her. Jay-Jay didn't care about her. He cared about me. If only he'd told me. If only I'd known.'

Privately, Oliver doubted James Hastings had cared about anyone but himself. Why else had he kept Rose Chen's identity a secret from her all these years? Her mother, a frail old woman whom Oliver had only seen once, and then only by chance, probably had more feelings for her estranged daughter than James Hastings had ever had. And his reasons for acknowledging his daughter now might have more to do with safeguarding his reputation than any sense of justice.

As for his wife and son in England...

Oliver could well imagine this turn of events had been a salutary blow to them. They couldn't have known of Rose Chen's existence either. But what did they know of James Hastings' dealings? That was the question. What did Rose Chen know, for that matter? How closely had she been trusted?

*   *   *

'You'll go with her, of course.'

Colonel Lightfoot's reaction was predictably positive. The burly professional soldier looked positively delighted at the prospect, his brows jerking excitedly, his bushy moustache quivering as he licked his fleshy lips.

'Will I?' Oliver leaned back in the chair across the desk, and propped one booted ankle across his knee. 'What if I don't want to go to England? What if I have other commitments here in the Colony?'

'Your only commitment is to me, Lynch,' began the colonel brusquely, and then, as if remembering that coercion had never worked with this particular operative, he allowed a cajoling note to enter his voice. 'Come on, Oliver,' he urged. 'We can't let the bastard get away with it. And until we know for certain how they're dealing with the stuff in England, we don't stand a rat's ass of making a conviction stick.'

Oliver considered the older man's words for a few moments, and then said, 'You believe Rose is involved, don't you?'

The colonel looked grim. 'Don't you?'

Oliver swung his leg to the floor and got up from his seat. Then, scowling, he paced across the floor. 'I suppose so.'

The colonel regarded him dourly. 'It doesn't bother you, does it?' He paused. 'You're not——' his mouth compressed as if he disliked having to ask the question '—in love with the girl, are you?'

Oliver's expression was sardonic now. 'No,' he said flatly. 'No, I'm not in love with her, Colonel. But—I suppose I care about what's going to happen to her. You can't sleep with a woman for almost six months without feeling some responsibility.'

The colonel's brows lowered above broad cheekbones, and he tapped an impatient finger on his desk. 'Might I remind you that Rose Chen probably knew exactly what she was doing? You may feel that you

educed her, but our sweet little dragon lady was desperate for your body.'

Oliver's lips twisted. 'You know that, of course.'

'I know that Hastings didn't trust you. I know he'd
have separated you if he could.'

Oliver frowned. 'He knew about us?'

The colonel sighed. 'Yes. Didn't I tell you?' But Oliver
could tell from his manner that he'd made a mistake.

He came to rest his hands on the colonel's desk,
pushing his face close to that of his superior. 'No, you
bloody well didn't,' he retorted, his stomach tightening
at the risks he had been taking. 'God, Colonel, if Rose
had been his mistress, Hastings could have had me
killed!'

'Oh, I think you're exaggerating,' muttered the
colonel, but they both knew life was cheap among the
criminal fraternity of Hong Kong. And if Hastings had
been the man they'd thought him, disposing of a possible
rival wouldn't have proved at all difficult.

Oliver swore, loudly and succinctly, before withdrawing his hands from the desk. Then, pushing them
into the pockets of his trousers, he gazed long and hos-
tilely at his employer. 'I'm dispensable, is that it?' he
asked at last, and Colonel Lightfoot uttered a frustrated
oath before getting up from his desk.

'No,' he said wearily, coming round the desk. 'For
God's sake, man, if I'd thought there was the slightest
danger——'

'Did you know Rose Chen was Hastings' daughter? I
mean—before his will was read?'

'I—suspected it.' The colonel sighed. 'Oliver, I'm sorry
if you think I should have been more honest with you.
But I couldn't risk your saying something that might
have jeopardised the operation.'

Oliver's mouth curled. 'Really?'

'Yes, really.' Colonel Lightfoot gazed at him unhappily, and then, when it became obvious that Oliver

wasn't going to buy that, he added heavily, 'We wanted Hastings to show his hand.'

'By killing me?' Oliver found he was amazingly indifferent to the suggestion.

'No, not by killing you.' Colonel Lightfoot conversely was growing increasingly desperate. 'Oliver—there was always a chance, a hope, that Hastings might attempt to recruit you.'

'To recruit me?'

'Of course.' The colonel nodded. 'If Rose Chen is involved, and, as I've told you, we think she is, isn't it a natural progression? She wanted you; she *wants* you. If, as we surmise, she refused to give you up, Hastings must have realised it was the only way to guarantee your silence.'

Oliver was silent for a moment. Then, he said, 'You hoped he would, didn't you?' He expelled his breath disbelievingly. 'You gave me this assignment because you thought I'd be the fall guy. Hey,' his voice harshened as he imitated the colonel's voice, 'why not give this one to Lynch? He's an ex-junkie, isn't he? He came out of Vietnam so screwed up, he didn't know what day it is. So what if Hastings grinds him down? Once a junkie, always a junkie, that's what I say!'

'That's not how it was,' insisted the colonel heavily. 'Dammit, Oliver, you know what I think of you; what I've always thought of you. You're a fine man, and a damn fine soldier. I gave you this assignment because you were the best man for the job. And if Hastings hadn't bought the farm we wouldn't be having this conversation.'

'No, we wouldn't.' Oliver flinched away from the reassuring hand the colonel attempted to lay on his shoulder. Then, with a shrug of his shoulders, he added, 'OK, Colonel, I'll go to London. I'll do what you want this time, but don't fix any more assignments for me, right? Suddenly I've got a yen to see Maple Falls again.

And, you know what? Even the idea of taking that job as an assistant district attorney doesn't sound so bad after all. I guess I'm getting old. Too old to be—jerked off—by someone like you!'

# CHAPTER TWO

'DEUCE.'

'It's game. The ball was out. I saw it.'

'Well, you would say that, wouldn't you?'

'The ball was out.'

'No, it wasn't.'

The twins' voices echoed intrusively from the tennis court, and Fliss, seated rather uncomfortably on the rim of the goldfish pond, thought how indifferent they seemed to their father's demise. But then they were only fifteen and, as far as she could gather, none of the Hastingses seemed particularly distraught about Mr Hastings' death. Bitter, yes; angry, certainly. But heart-broken, distressed, grief-stricken—no.

'Isn't it absolutely bloody sickening?'

Her fiancé, Robert, rocking rather more comfortably on the swing-set, set the cushioned seat moving at a nauseating pace. Fliss, who had been envying him his position only moments before, was glad she wasn't sitting beside him now. She was sure she would have been sick.

'I feel sorry for your mother,' she said, after a moment, not quite knowing how to answer him. The discovery that Mr Hastings had been leading a double life was embarrassing, no doubt, and Mrs Hastings couldn't avoid being the brunt of some gossip in the cloistered environs of Sutton Magna.

Robert was unsympathetic. 'Why feel sorry for her?' he demanded unfeelingly, revealing a side of his character Fliss had been totally unaware of until recently. 'If it weren't for her, the old man wouldn't have looked elsewhere for his pleasures. She's a cold fish, my mother. Or hadn't you noticed?'

In actual fact, Fliss had noticed. Her own dealings with Robert's mother had never been exactly friendly. Amanda Hastings didn't encourage any kind of closeness between the girl her only son was going to marry and herself, and although Fliss was a frequent visitor to the house she didn't feel at home there.

Nevertheless . . .

'Imagine,' Robert went on in the same bitter vein, 'having a Chinese mistress! God, do you suppose she'll bring a whole gaggle of orientals with her? The Chinese are big on family ties, aren't they? Dammit, Fliss, how could the old bastard do this to us?'

Fliss tried to be practical. 'Mr Davis didn't say anything about the girl's having a family,' she pointed out, but Robert wasn't convinced.

'Huh, Davis,' he grunted. 'What does he know? Where's the girl's mother? That's what I'd like to know. Is she expecting a share of this, as well as her daughter?'

'So far as we know there only is—Rose Chen? Is that right?' replied Fliss, more calmly than she felt. 'The girl's probably an orphan. That's why your father felt some responsibility for her.'

'But what about us?' protested Robert. 'Liz and Dody and me? You don't seem to realise, Fliss, my father has left her half of everything. The trading company; the shops; even this house! What if she wants to sell it? Where are we going to live?'

Fliss could see it was a problem, though for herself she wouldn't be sorry if she and Robert didn't have to live at the house after they were married. Sutton Grange, as it was rather pretentiously called, was not an attractive example of Victorian architecture, and she much preferred the old vicarage, where she and her father lived.

Not that she and Robert could move in there, she conceded, in a momentary digression. Although Robert and

the Reverend Matthew Hayton tolerated one another's
company, she couldn't deny they had little in common.
Since her mother had died some years ago her father
had developed an interest in local history, and every
moment he had free from his duties as the village clergyman he spent researching the parish records. He had no
interest in sailing, or horse-racing, or playing golf. Or
in fine arts either, Fliss conceded.

As far as Fliss was concerned, her mother's death,
while she was still at university actually, had left a void
in both their lives no one else could fill. And because
her father obviously needed someone, not just to take
over his wife's role in the community, but also to act as
his secretary, she had found herself accepting that position, and abandoning any ambitions she had had to
have a career of her own.

She had never really regretted it, even though the life
she led in this Buckinghamshire backwater was vastly
different from the life led by most young women of her
age. At twenty-six she enjoyed an almost bucolic
existence, and only since her engagement to Robert
Hastings had she had the kind of social life he had always
taken for granted.

Which was why, she supposed, Mrs Hastings had not
been exactly enthusiastic about the match. Robert's
mother had no doubt expected him to marry someone
from a similar background to their own; someone whose
father was fairly wealthy, or whose family had a title.
A daughter-in-law she could present to the world, a
daughter-in-law she could be proud of.

Fliss knew she was none of those things. Vicars'
daughters were not titled, and they were not wealthy,
and as for Mrs Hastings being proud of her, well . . . She
shrugged her slim shoulders. She had often wondered
what Robert saw in her, what had possibly persuaded
him to ask her out?

They had met at the village fair last autumn. Fliss had been in charge of the book stall as usual, spending at least part of the time examining the merchandise, indulging herself shamelessly in any and every volume. Books were Fliss's one weakness, and she invariably bought the books herself if no one else was interested.

Why Robert had been there at all, she couldn't imagine. The noise and bustle of a village fair didn't seem his scene at all. Though he had been interested in the bric-a-brac stall, she remembered. Probably in the hope of snaring a bargain. Mr Hastings owned several fine art shops, and, although no one could confuse Mrs Darcy's pot dogs and stuffed owls with fine art, just occasionally a piece of crystal or a chipped Crown Derby plate found its way on to the stall.

She had been admiring an old copy of poems by Lord Tennyson when Robert had stopped at her stall. His appearance had surprised her, but Fliss seldom got flustered. Indeed, she was of the opinion that she was one of those people who didn't have it in them to feel any uncontrollable surge of excitement, and although her golden eyes widened she was perfectly composed.

And, unaware as she was of it, it was that air of cool untouchability that caught and held Robert Hastings' interest. That, and the fact that she was tall—taller than average—and unfashionably curvaceous, with full, rounded breasts, and long, shapely legs. She also had a mass of sun-streaked brown hair, that hung quite untidily about her shoulders. In short, she was an extremely feminine example of her breed, and if her nose was too long, and her mouth too wide, the overall impression was delightful.

So much so that Robert, a fairly discerning connoisseur of her sex, was instantly attracted, and showed it. Much to her father's dismay, she was sure, he had spent the remainder of the afternoon hanging round her stall, and when the fair was over he'd spirited her off to the pub for a drink.

Fliss, who seldom drank anything stronger than the communion wine, found herself with a cocktail glass on one hand and an ardent suitor on the other, and for once she was glad she wasn't easily excited. Another girl might have been bowled over by the fact that probably the most eligible bachelor for miles around was giving her his undivided attention. As it was, Fliss found it all rather amusing, and not at all worrying as her father seemed to think.

And, although Robert might have expected a different response from a young woman without any obvious advantages, he had soon had to accept that, if he wanted to get anywhere with Fliss, he would have to be a lot less arrogant, and a lot more patient. And he had been. To her immense surprise and amazement, he admitted to having fallen in love with her, and, as an abortive affair when she was in college was all Fliss had to compare her own affection for him with, she had come to the eventual conclusion that she must love him too. Certainly she liked being with him. He was warm and affectionate, and he made her feel good.

And, after a winter in which Robert had sustained his assault on her emotions, she had finally agreed to his announcing their engagement. The only disadvantage she had found since that event was Robert was now twice as eager to consummate—as he put it—their relationship; only consummation, as a vicar's daughter, meant something rather different to Fliss...

'I should think,' she said carefully now, desperate to escape the implications of that particular thought for the present, and returning to the subject of the house, 'that your mother might welcome the opportunity to find somewhere smaller.' Knowing Mrs Hastings as she did, she doubted this was really true, but she pressed on anyway. 'I mean, now that your father's—dead——' she licked her upper lip delicately '—she won't have to host all those country weekends and dinner parties that Mr Hastings wished upon her.'

Robert stared at her impatiently. 'You're not serious.'

Fliss smoothed slender fingers over a bare shoulder, exposed by the bootlace straps of her sundress, and gave a little shrug. 'Why not?'

'Why not?' Robert was briefly diverted by the unknowing sensuality of her action, but he eventually shook his head as if to clear it, and exclaimed irritably, 'As I shall be running the company from now on, this should have been my house, not my mother's. And as for entertaining, I should have been hosting all social occasions from now on.'

'Yes, I know, but——'

'This was going to be our home, yours and mine,' he added grimly. 'We would have carried on the family tradition.'

Fliss had been afraid of that, and she wondered if it would be too disloyal of her to feel some relief that the prospect had been put in jeopardy. Was Robert suggesting they would have lived here with his mother and his twin sisters? Dear God, she couldn't have done that. It simply wasn't on.

She also forbore from pointing out that the 'family tradition' he spoke about was barely twenty years old. As far as the villagers were concerned, they were still newcomers. Besides, James Hastings' indiscretions were bound to put a halt to any delusions of grandeur.

'Well,' she said evenly, 'whatever happens, I think we should start married life in a home of our own. Not here. We should choose our own place. Somewhere we can decorate and furnish as we like.'

Robert brought the swing to a sudden halt. 'What's wrong with the Grange?'

'Nothing.' Fliss realised she had to be tactful here. 'But this is your mother's home—at least, for the present.

And—and it's Liz and Dody's home, too. Haven't you just said so?'

Robert frowned, the deepening cleft between his blonde brows drawing attention to the fairness of his skin. Even in the height of summer, Robert's flesh never changed colour. The sun might burn it sometimes, but he never got a tan.

Conversely, Fliss's skin was of that creamy variety that browned easily. Unlike her hair, which was bleached by the sun's rays, her arms and legs took on the healthy glow of honey. A fact that dismayed Mrs Hastings, who protected her own skin with almost fanatical zeal.

'I don't want to move,' Robert declared now, his gaze moving over the acres of formal garden to where his sisters still squabbled on the tennis court. And it was true, the neatly trimmed hedges and rose gardens were a delight, particularly at this time of year.

'Maybe you won't have to,' Fliss offered, stifling for the moment her own misgivings about living at Sutton Grange. 'You're endowing this woman—Rose Chen— with characteristics you can't possibly know she possesses. She may be just as upset by the situation as you are. Didn't you say Mr Davis was of the opinion that she hadn't known the truth before your father's will was read?'

Robert shrugged his shoulders. He was a tall man, inclined to sturdiness, and he had played rugby in his youth. In fact he was still a formidable opponent on the field. Yet, for all that, there was a certain weakness about his chin that had nothing to do with his good looks, and a sulkiness about his mouth that was presently all too apparent.

'You don't really believe that, Fliss, do you?' he asked, and although his expression hadn't changed his voice was softer. 'Oh, hell, and this was supposed to be the happiest year of our lives. We were getting married at Christmas. I don't know what's going to happen now.'

He held out his hand towards her, and, not sorry to leave the concrete rim of the pond, Fliss allowed him to pull her on to his lap. The swing rocked gently now as he nuzzled his face against her shoulder, and she wished there were something she could say to ease his troubled thoughts.

'There's plenty of time,' she comforted, putting her arm about his neck and cradling his head against her breast. Really, she thought, there had been occasions lately when she'd felt more like Robert's mother than his girlfriend. He could appear totally helpless at times.

Well, perhaps that was an exaggeration, she conceded quickly, feeling his hand invading the camisole neckline of her dress. She shouldn't mistake petulance for vulnerability. Robert was usually fairly adept at getting what he wanted, and who knew that he wouldn't soon have the Chinese girl, his half-sister, Rose Chen, eating out of his hand?

She was about to put his hand away when one of the twins, Fliss thought it was Dody, came tearing across the lawn, and achieved her objective for her. 'Rob! Rob!' Dody was calling, her plump adolescent legs pumping urgently inside her biker's shorts. 'Rob, Mummy says you've got to come up to the terrace immediately. That woman's arrived! Our—*sister*! And she's brought ever such a gorgeous hunk with her!'

Even allowing for Dody's tendency towards exaggeration, Fliss had to admit that Oliver Lynch was one of the most disturbing men she had ever laid eyes on. *The* most disturbing, she suspected, although that seemed a little disloyal towards Robert.

Nevertheless, Oliver Lynch did present a most imposing presence, and even Robert, at six feet exactly, had to look up at the older man. And he was much older, Fliss decided, using that acknowledgement as a means of reparation. He might not look it, but he had to be forty-one or -two, at least. To a polite question from Mrs Hastings, he had admitted to spending some time in Vietnam, and that war had been over for twenty years or more.

But the fact remained, he was disturbing, and attractive. He wasn't handsome, as Robert was handsome. His features were too strongly moulded for that. But there was something very masculine—very sexual—about deep-set eyes, hollow cheekbones and a thin-lipped mouth. In some ways it was a cruel face, enhanced by the unconventional length of his hair. Long and black, he pushed it back with a careless hand, the rolled-back sleeves of his shirt exposing a long white scar that marked the flesh from elbow to wrist.

He not only looked disturbing, he disturbed her, thought Fliss uneasily, not really understanding why this should be so. She tried to tell herself it was because of Robert, that his association with the woman, Rose Chen, made him as much of a threat as she was, but that wasn't it. If she was honest she would admit he disturbed her in a much more personal, purely visceral way. Just looking at him caused a curious pain to stir, down deep in her stomach. And when Rose Chen touched his arm, or his hand, as she did frequently—as if she needed to display her possession—Fliss looked away, as if the image offended her.

Of course it was all quite silly, she reproved herself half mockingly. She didn't even know why she was giving him a second thought. It wasn't as if she had any desire to change her comfortable existence. However petulant Robert might be, he was also tender and kind, and incredibly patient. Not characteristics she could apply to Oliver Lynch, she was sure.

From her position, curled up on one of the cushioned lounges at the far end of the terrace, she was able to observe the behaviour of the other people present without drawing attention to herself. They were all being amazingly civil, she thought, remembering how bitter Robert had been before their arrival. But then his mother hadn't met Oliver Lynch then, nor been seduced by his southern courtesy and charm.

Forcing her attention away from Oliver Lynch, she wondered what her fiancé was really thinking. Tea had been served, and presently he was exchanging pleasantries about their journey with the woman, Rose Chen. No one could be more polite, or more facile, than an Englishman, Fliss reflected drily. Unless it was an American. There was no denying that Oliver Lynch was displaying his share of diplomacy.

She forced her mind back to the Chinese woman. Rose Chen—was that really her name?—was older, too, than they had expected. Was that why they were all being so civil to her? Had the realisation that she was not a young girl reassured Amanda Hastings of her own credibility?

Whatever, it was obvious that Mr Hastings' affair with Rose Chen's mother must have happened at least thirty years ago. Maybe thirty-five. Fliss couldn't be absolutely certain. And if that was the case, Robert hadn't even been born when his father took a mistress.

'Do you think she's his mistress?'

The whispered words so closely following Fliss's thoughts, caused her to gaze at one of Robert's sisters blankly.

'Who?' she answered, in an undertone, hoping no one else was listening to their exchange, and the twin—Liz, she thought—rolled her eyes impatiently.

'Oliver Lynch, of course,' she hissed, glancing surreptitiously over her shoulder. 'Don't tell me you haven't thought about it, too. I saw you looking at him earlier.'

Fliss was glad the vine-clad roof that overhung the terrace cast her face into shadow. Liz's words had caused a faint tinge of hot colour to enter her cheeks, and she wouldn't have liked to have to explain it to anyone else. Contrary to what people of your age believe, older women do not speculate about other people's sexual habits as soon as they've been introduced,' she replied quellingly. 'He could be her husband, as far as we know.' Though that caused another discomforting flutter in her stomach. 'It's nothing to do with us.'

'Older women!' said Liz disparagingly, picking up on the one topic she could argue with. 'You're not old, Fliss, and you know it.'

'I'm twenty-six, and sometimes I feel old enough to be your mother,' retorted Fliss drily. 'In any case, that has nothing to do with it, I'm not interested in Mr Lynch.'

'Mummy is.' Liz tipped her head defiantly. 'She hasn't taken her eyes off him since he and—Rose Chen—got out of the car. Did you see the car he was driving, by the way? I think it's a Ferrari. It's long and low and really mean. Dody was nearly drooling!'

Fliss shook her head. 'Liz! Your father's only been dead just over three weeks. Show a little respect.'

Liz grimaced. 'I'm not being disrespectful,' she argued. 'Haven't you noticed the way Mummy's stationed herself at his elbow? How old do you think he is, anyway? Eight—ten years younger than she is?'

'Liz!' Fliss was getting very impatient with this conversation. 'Go and find someone else to pester, will you? You're giving me a headache.'

'That's because you're frustrated,' Liz retaliated, in parting, and Fliss was so glad to see her go that she didn't dispute it.

Instead, she uncoiled her legs from under her and reached for the cooling cup of tea resting on a nearby end table. She wished she could go, she thought. Robert didn't need her at the moment, and she had no doubt she would hear all about his conversation with Rose Chen. To distraction, probably, she mused ruefully, recalling that since his father's will had been read it had become almost the sole topic of conversation. She sympathised with him; or course she did. But surely half the company was enough to satisfy even the most prodigal of heirs. She appreciated the things that money could buy, but she couldn't understand why some men were prepared to sacrifice everything, even their self-respect, in the pursuit of great wealth. Her father said it had to do with power, with the power that money brought. But Fliss—probably due to her father's influence—had little use for either.

'Are you?'

The lazily spoken enquiry was so unexpected that Fliss almost spilled her tea. She had been so absorbed with her thoughts that she had been unaware of anyone's approach, least of all that of the man who had eased his long length into the chair beside hers.

'I beg your pardon?' she said, glad to find that for all her trepidation she sounded pleasantly composed. She crossed her legs, swiftly gathering together the skirt of her dress when its wraparound folds threatened to part. 'Did you say something?'

'I said—are you?' Oliver Lynch repeated levelly, though she could tell from his expression that he didn't believe she hadn't heard him the first time. With an errant breeze lifting the ends of his dark hair, and his muscled forearms resting along his thighs, thighs that had parted to accommodate the booted feet set squarely on the floor of the terrace, he was too close for comfort. The neckline of his navy silk shirt was open to display a disturbing glimpse of body hair as well, and Fliss thought he looked like a predator, his casual air of relaxation as spurious as his smile.

'Am I what?' she asked politely, returning her fragile cup to its saucer. She gave him an enquiring look. 'I fear you have me at a disadvantage, Mr—er—Lynch.'

Oliver Lynch's thin lips parted. 'I doubt that, ma'am,' he countered, with equal formality. 'The kid accused you of being frustrated. I wondered if you agreed.'

'Did you?' Fliss's breath escaped with a rush. She didn't believe it for a moment. 'I don't really think you expect me to answer that question.' She glanced along the terrace and saw Robert's mother watching them with undisguised hostility, and inwardly groaned. 'Um—is this your first visit to England?'

'No.'

He was non-committal, curiously pale eyes—wolf's eyes, she decided imaginatively—assessing her appearance intently. Was he only trying to embarrass her? Or was he bored by their company, and eager for diversion? Whatever the prognosis, she wished he'd chosen someone else to practise on.

'You're an American,' she observed now, striving for a neutral topic. 'But you live in Hong Kong. Do you have business interests there, too?'

'You could say that,' he responded carelessly, and she immediately felt as if she was being unpardonably inquisitive. But, heavens, what was she supposed to say to a man who was so obviously out of her realm of experience? She had never considered herself particularly good at small talk, and his kind of verbal baiting left her feeling gauche.

'Do you live in Sutton Magna, Miss Hayton?' he asked after a moment, and Fliss was relieved he hadn't made some other mocking comment. 'Mandy says you're going to marry Robert,' he added, with a slight edge to his voice. 'Is that right?'

*Mandy?*

It took Fliss a second to realise he was talking about Mrs Hastings. She had never heard Amanda Hastings referred to as 'Mandy' before. 'Um—yes,' she answered hurriedly. 'To both your questions. My father is the local clergyman. Maybe you and—your friend would like to visit the church while you're here. It's a Norman church, and parts of it date back to the twelfth century.'

'I'm not a tourist, Miss Hayton.' Oliver Lynch's tone
*as vaguely hostile now, and Fliss wondered what she
*ad said to annoy him. She had only been trying to make
*onversation. There was no need for him to be rude.

But her innate good manners wouldn't allow her to
*ut him in his place as she should, so 'I'm sorry,' she
*aid courteously. 'I didn't mean to imply you were.'

Oliver Lynch's eyes darkened, a curious phenomenon
*at caused the pupils to dilate and almost obscure the
*ale irises. 'Forget it,' he said, his low voice harsh and
*mpatient. 'I'm an ignorant bastard. I guess I'm not used
* mixing in polite company.'

Now what was she supposed to make of that? Fliss's
*ongue moved rather nervously over her upper lip. She
*asn't sure how to answer him, and she wished Robert's
*mother would stop scowling at her and come to her
*escue.

'Er—let me get you some more tea, Mr Lynch,' she
*entured, relieved at the inspiration. 'It really is a hot
*ternoon, and I'm sure you must be thirsty.'

'I am,' he agreed, his pupils resuming their normal
*ze, and a humorous grin lifting the corners of his
*outh. 'But——' he laid a hand on her bare arm as she
*ould have got to her feet '—not for tea! If there's a
*eer lying around here, I'll take it. But not more of the
*kewarm—stuff—I was offered earlier.'

Fliss jerked her arm back as if he'd burned her. And
*deed, the sensation his hand had induced on her flesh
*as not unlike that description. His fingers, lean and
*rd and *cool*, had left an indelible imprint. So much
* that, for a moment, she had hardly been aware of
*hat he was saying.

Instead, she found herself wondering how it would
*el to have his hands on her body; and not just her
*mbs, which were already melting at the thought. But
* her waist; her hips; her breasts. She caught her breath.
*e idea that he might also touch her intimately was a

fascinating prospect, and it took Robert's voice to arouse her from the dangerous spiral of her thoughts.

'I see you've introduced yourself to my fiancée, Lynch. What have you been saying to make her look so guilty?'

The American rose in one lithe easy movement, in no way daunted by the faint edge of animosity in the Englishman's tone. 'Oh—we were discussing the relative merits of tea, among other things,' he replied, not altogether untruthfully. 'As a stranger in your country, I'm not accustomed to the—customs.'

Robert seemed to realise there was something rather ambiguous about this statement, but short of asking what he meant outright there was little he could say. 'Well, I hope Fliss has satisfied your curiosity,' he remarked tightly. 'Naturally, we'll all do what we can to make your stay as pleasant as possible.'

Oliver Lynch's smile didn't reach his eyes, but there was genuine warmth in his voice as he replied, 'Your fiancée has been most charming. I hope you appreciate her.'

'Oh, I do.' Even if Fliss had not been thinking of getting to her feet at that moment, she felt sure the possessive hand Robert placed about her arm would have achieved it. There was anger now, as well as proprietorial ownership, in the way he drew her up beside him, sliding his arm about her waist, as if to underline his claim. 'Fliss is my one weakness,' he said, though there was little leniency in his voice. 'She can wrap me round her finger any time she likes.' And, bending his head towards her, he bestowed a prolonged kiss on her startled mouth.

If Fliss hadn't been embarrassed before, she was now, with Oliver Lynch's pale eyes observing their every move. If it weren't so fanciful she'd have said he knew what she was thinking. Though not what she'd thought before, please God, she prayed with some conviction.

'You're a very lucky man,' Lynch remarked now, into the vacuum that Fliss felt was as visible as it was heard. If Robert had intended to disconcert the other man, he was going to be sadly disappointed. Oliver Lynch was only amused by her fiancé's behaviour. Amused at, and slightly contemptuous of, his attempt to display possession.

# CHAPTER THREE

'But why do we have to have separate rooms?' asked Rose Chen impatiently. 'It's not as if we have to keep our relationship a secret or anything. I know you've always insisted on keeping your own apartment in Hong Kong, but surely this is different? We are travelling together.'

'I've told you: I need my own space,' said Oliver shortly, growing tired of the argument they had been having since they booked into the hotel.

They were staying at the Moathouse in Market Risborough, which was the nearest town to Sutton Magna. The night before, Rose had stayed with her father's agent in Fulham, and Oliver had occupied a room in a small hotel off Piccadilly.

Rose heaved a deep breath now. 'Have I done something wrong?' she demanded. 'I thought our first meeting with the Hastingses went off rather well. At least they aren't openly hostile. It was a brilliant idea of yours to make the first move so informal. They could hardly throw us out without creating quite a fuss.' She paused. 'Though I did detect some undercurrents, didn't you?'

'Maybe.'

Oliver was non-committal. In truth, he hadn't devoted as much attention to the reasons why they had gone to Sutton Grange as he should. From the moment he'd laid eyes on Felicity Hayton he'd been hard pressed to keep his mind on anything else. Her cool, honey-blonde beauty had done forgotten things to his nervous system. Just thinking about how her skin felt—smooth and soft beneath his fingers—still caused a definite tightening in his groin.

Which was fairly pathetic, and he knew it. Ever since the youthful marriage he had contracted in college had ended with a 'Dear John' letter while he was in Vietnam, he had had no use for emotional relationships. There had been women, of course—plenty of them, he acknowledged without conceit—but they had served their purpose and been forgotten. He supposed his association with Rose Chen was the closest thing to a permanent relationship he had had since his teenage years.

But it was just a job, and one which he sometimes despised himself for. He liked Rose, he admired her spirit, and sometimes he'd even felt some affection towards her. But he didn't love her. He doubted he had ever really loved anyone.

'Something is wrong, isn't it?' Rose was nothing if not persistent. 'What did Robert say to you? He wasn't awkward or anything, was he? I know his mother was a real pain, but I thought he kept his cool.'

Except where his fiancée was concerned, thought Oliver drily, remembering the way the other man had dragged Felicity—*Fliss*—up from her chair and practically savaged her. Oliver could still feel the fury he had felt when Hastings had put his hands upon her. He hadn't cared at that moment whether the younger man had known of his father's dealings or not. All he'd wanted to do was put his hands about the other man's thick neck and squeeze, and squeeze, and squeeze...

'He's a runt,' declared Oliver succinctly, his own feelings briefly getting the better of him. He knew it wouldn't do to alert Rose Chen to the dislike he felt for her half-brother, but it felt good to voice his contempt just the same.

'You think so?'

Naturally, Rose Chen was interested in his opinion, and Oliver had to quickly fabricate a reason for his remark. 'I gathered from his mother that he doesn't like work,' he said dismissively. 'If even half what she says is true, he seems to spend most of his time either at the race-track or on the golfcourse.'

'I see.' Rose Chen caught her lower lip between her teeth. 'That could be useful, couldn't it? If Robert isn't too familiar with running the business, he may not be so opposed to my taking charge.'

'In a pig's eye,' said Oliver, wondering if Rose could really be as gullible as she liked to appear. Personally he didn't believe it for a moment. She was James Hastings' daughter; she must know what there was at stake.

Rose Chen lifted her slim shoulders now. She'd worn a cream silk suit to go to Sutton Magna, but she'd shed the jacket since she got back, and her arms were bare. Her hair was short, moulding her shapely head like a black cap. Her small breasts were taut against her silk vest, and the short skirt of the suit showed her legs to advantage. She was small and exotic and sexy, but Oliver felt no attraction as she preened before his gaze.

The trouble was, he was comparing her dainty appearance to the long-legged Englishwoman he had met on the Hastingses' terrace. And, although Fliss didn't possess Rose Chen's sophistication, she was infinitely more feminine. Tall, easily five feet eight, he guessed, and not thin in the way most women these days were thin, but supple, and shapely, with breasts a man could die for. She was elegant and classy, with legs that went on forever. Not at all like the women he was used to, with her golden skin and hair...

'Whatever,' Rose Chen murmured carelessly, lifting her arms and cupping the back of her neck. Her oval eyes sought Oliver's as he lounged against the writing table. 'I think I'll take a shower. D'you want to join me?'

Oliver straightened. 'No, thanks,' he said swiftly, and then tempered his refusal with a brief smile. 'I've got some unpacking to do, and I thought I might call home.' He grimaced. 'It's cheaper ringing from London than it is from the Far East.'

Rose Chen hid her impatience badly. 'We will dine together, I assume? You won't be too tired? Or suffering from jet-lag?'

Oliver strolled towards the door. 'I'll try to keep awake,' he responded over his shoulder. 'Shall we say seven-thirty? We'd better not make it too late. Hastings is picking you up at eight o'clock tomorrow morning, isn't he?'

'He's picking *us* up,' amended Rose Chen tersely. 'I want you to come with me, Lee. You're so much better at reading people's faces than I am.'

Oliver acknowledged her remark with lazy indulgence, but as soon as the door had closed behind him he frowned. He knew that as far as the colonel was concerned things could not be going better. The old man had actually asked Oliver to try and get inside the Hastings offices and find out as much as he could about distribution and so on. And, while accompanying Rose Chen was not quite what he had had in mind, it might be possible to use the visit to his own advantage.

He called Hong Kong while he was waiting for room service to deliver the bottle of Scotch he'd ordered. It was already the early hours of the following morning there, but he guessed Colonel Lightfoot would be waiting for his call. Rose Chen had no idea that 'calling home' were his own code words for keeping in touch with the agency. So far as she was concerned, he was keeping in touch with his family. And, doubtless he'd do that, too, if only to cover himself. Besides, his mother would appreciate it.

Colonel Lightfoot's voice was barely drowsy. If he had been asleep, he was one of those people who was instantly awake. Oliver guessed he'd half expected him to call the previous evening. But until he'd encountered Robert Hastings he'd really had nothing to report.

'The family,' said the colonel, after Oliver's initial impressions had been aired. 'Do you think his wife is aware of what's been going on?'

'Difficult to say.' Oliver wasn't sure what he thought about Amanda Hastings. The woman had come on to him, but that might have been her way of sounding him out. She had certainly been curious about his relationship with Rose Chen, but once again she might have had her own reasons for asking so many questions.

'You say you're going to the company's offices tomorrow?' The colonel didn't waste time on speculation. 'I don't think anyone will make any mistakes while you're around, but you may be able to assess whether Rose Chen has any authority.'

Oliver absorbed this without comment. Unless the upheaval of learning she was Robert Hastings' daughter had made Rose Chen more vulnerable, he doubted he would learn anything from her behaviour. As far as business was concerned, Rose Chen had been the ideal employee: she had respected her employer's confidence, and never betrayed any of his secrets, even in the heat of passion.

'Of course, it's her reaction to Robert Hastings we're interested in,' the colonel went on doggedly. 'The apparent animosity between them may be just a front. We can't be absolutely sure that neither of them knew of the other's existence before Hastings cashed his chips.'

Oliver didn't argue, but personally he was fairly sure they hadn't. Even without Rose Chen's response he had sensed that, for all his apparent affability towards his half-sister, Robert Hastings was inwardly seething.

There had been that moment with his fiancée, for example. He hadn't just been reacting to the fact that another man was showing her some attention—though if he'd known Oliver's thoughts he might have been; there had been anger and barely suppressed violence in his actions. And it hadn't been just because he was a man. It was who he was that mattered. As far as Hastings was concerned, he—Oliver—was irrevocably linked with Rose Chen.

'You're not saying a lot,' Colonel Lightfoot commented at last, and Oliver gathered his drifting thoughts.

'There's not a lot to say,' he responded evenly. 'I'll be in touch again when I've got something to report.'

'Right.' The colonel hesitated. 'You wouldn't go soft on me, would you, Lynch? I'd hate to see that solid gold reputation sullied because you've let your—sexual urges—rule your head. I know you care about the woman. But don't think that warning her will do her any good.'

The short laugh Oliver uttered then was ironic. If only Archie knew, he thought wryly. It wasn't his Chinese nemesis the colonel had to worry about. It was a cool, innocent Englishwoman, Oliver was remembering. With skin as sweet as honey, and hair as fine as silk...

'And you say Robert isn't coming to terms with the situation?' Matthew Hayton remarked thoughtfully, looking at his daughter over the rims of his spectacles. 'Well, I don't really see what choice he's got.'

'Nor do I,' averred Fliss energetically. 'The woman's identity's been verified and, if that wasn't enough, she's shown a remarkable aptitude for filling the void left by Mr Hastings' death. Honestly, Rose Chen knows more about the business than Robert ever has. She's a natural organiser, and she certainly gets things done.'

'Which is probably another reason why Robert objects to her presence,' declared the Reverend Matthew Hayton drily. 'I mean, you can't deny that Robert seldom showed a great deal of interest in the company when his

father was alive. He spent more time playing golf and
sailing his yacht than he ever did in the office.'

'Robert's always maintained that his father never gave
him any responsibility,' Fliss exclaimed loyally. 'And
after all, Mr Hastings was only in his fifties. Who'd have
thought he'd die so young? He never seemed to have
much stress in his life. Though I suppose if he was leading
a double life there must have been some strain.'

'Hardly a double life, Felicity.' Her father was the only
person who ever called her by her given name, and now
he viewed his daughter with some misgivings. 'We can't
really speculate about Hastings' life in Hong Kong. And
if neither Robert nor——'

'Rose Chen?'

'—nor Rose Chen knew of each other's existence, the
affair—if that was what it was—must have been over
some time ago.'

Fliss nodded. 'I suppose so.'

'In any event, it's not our concern, Felicity, and I hope
you don't encourage Robert to criticise his father's behaviour.' He pushed his spectacles back up his nose, and
returned his attention to the sermon he was trying to
compose. 'People who live in glass houses, Felicity. Need
I say more?'

Fliss snorted. 'I don't encourage Robert to talk about
his father, Dad, but he does it anyway.' She grimaced.
'He talks about little else. Oh, and he moans about Oliver
Lynch's influence on Rose Chen, as well. Apparently,
she's insisted he sits in on their meetings—like a skeleton
at the feast, according to Rob.'

Matthew Hayton looked up again. 'Oliver Lynch?' he
frowned. 'Oh, that American you said had accompanied her. What is he? Her accountant? Her
solicitor?'

Fliss shuffled the pile of reference books she had been
tidying, and gave a careless shrug of her shoulders.
'Her—partner, I think,' she said, bending her head so

her father shouldn't see the colour that had stained her cheeks at his words.

'Her partner?' Matthew Hayton frowned. 'You mean, he has a share in the business, too?'

'No.' Fliss wished she hadn't mentioned Oliver Lynch at all. 'He's her—boyfriend, I believe. At least, Robert says she can't keep her hands off him.'

'I see.' Her father arched his brows that were several shades lighter than his daughter's. 'And Robert thinks this man exercises some undue influence on his—sister, is that right?'

'Well—something like that,' agreed Fliss uncomfortably. 'No one seems to know what he does exactly. He doesn't appear to have a job, and—well, Robert thinks he must be living off Rose Chen.' She hesitated and then added reluctantly, 'He certainly wears expensive clothes for someone without any obvious means of support.'

Matthew Hayton took off his spectacles now, and gave his daughter a reproving look. 'Felicity, this is all hearsay, isn't it? I doubt very much whether Robert has actually asked Rose Chen what this man—Lynch, did you say?—does.'

'No, but——'

'He may be a man of substance. He may have independent means. I don't think you should immediately assume he's some kind of—what's the word?—pimp? Just because Robert's feeling betrayed by his father's deception.'

'No,' said Fliss again, but with rather less emphasis. And, after all, her father had a point. Robert really did know nothing about Oliver Lynch. If she was perfectly honest, she'd have to admit that she'd only sympathised with him because she'd been intimidated by Oliver Lynch's tall, dark presence.

'So, what did you think of the man?' Reverend Hayton prompted now, and Fliss realised that her careless words

had got her into even deeper water. The last thing she
wanted to do was discuss Oliver Lynch with her father.
Particularly as her reaction to him had been so disturbingly confused.

'He seemed—very nice,' she said carefully, avoiding
making any statement that might initiate a follow-up.
'Um—I think I'll go over to the church. I promised Mrs
Rennie I'd help her with the flowers.'

Her father looked as if he might have some further
comment to make, and she balled her fists in the pockets
of the linen trousers she was wearing as she waited for
the verbal axe to fall. But all Matthew Hayton said was,
'Ask Mr Brewitt to check on the communion wine, if
you see him,' before pushing his spectacles back in place
and returning to his sermon.

Outside the pleasantly cool environs of her father's
study, the air was hot and decidedly humid. At this time
of year, any long spell of hot weather was usually followed by a bout of thunderstorms, and the sky had that
ominous overcast sheen that often heralded bad weather.

Other than that, the village looked rather pretty at the
moment. The cottage gardens were filled with every kind
of flower imaginable, and sunflowers and hollyhocks rose
thickly above the rest. There were geraniums, too, in
great numbers, spilling from every hedge and border,
and tumbling riotously from stone urns and planters.
Only the lawns looked rather parched, because sprinklers
had been forbidden.

The vicarage garden was no different from the rest,
and Fliss, who invariably ended up having to do the
weeding herself, viewed its dried beds with some misgivings. The church did employ a caretaker, part of
whose duties was to keep the grass neat in the
churchyard, and to look after the rather large gardens
of the vicarage. Church fêtes were always held on the
back lawn, and it was important to keep the weeds at
bay. But Mr Hood was really too old now to do all that

was needed. Even with a tractor mower, he found it hard
to pull his weight. Not that the Reverend would ever
force him to retire, thought Fliss affectionately. Not as
long as Mr Hood wanted to work. Until he chose to
retire, the job was his.

Walking up the gravel path to the vestry door, Fliss
lifted the weight of her hair from her neck with a slightly
weary hand. She really ought to have her hair cut, she
thought ruefully. Or confine it permanently in a braid.
Having long hair might look nice, but it certainly wasn't
easy to handle. And it could be rather tiresome at this
time of year.

Still, it wasn't really her hair that was making her feel
so tired all of a sudden. The truth was, she wasn't
sleeping well. These warm, humid nights left her feeling
limp, not rested, and the problems Robert was having
were creating troubles for her, too.

Ever since their engagement, Robert's attitude towards
her had become more and more possessive, and she
wondered if it was because she had so far evaded giving
in to his demands that he was so aggressive. Since Rose
Chen came on the scene he had become increasingly persistent, and he was no longer willing to make com-
promises. He wanted her, he said. Not at some nebulous
date in the future, but now. Nothing in his life was certain
any more, and he needed her with him to keep him sane.

Her protestations that she was *with* him, that possession was nine-tenths in the mind anyway, didn't persuade him. How could he feel she was really his when
she drew the line at the bedroom door? he asked. When
two people loved one another, there should be no lines,
no barriers.

Of course, there were other arguments: that she was
prudish and old-fashioned—arguments she couldn't
really defend. Perhaps she was both those things, but
there wasn't much she could do about it. Sex had never
figured highly in her thoughts.

And the truth was, although she liked Robert, and cared about him, after her experience at college she didn't know if she had it in her to feel any more deeply than that. There were women—she had read about them in magazines—who were happily married, with a handful of children, who'd never known what real passion was. The importance of feeling loved, of feeling wanted, was what they cared about. Orgasm—a word which was freely bandied about today, and which her father abhorred—was not something she was eager to experience. She was sure it was vastly over-rated; something men had introduced to try and get their way.

She sighed. Not that that conclusion in any way solved her problem. She still had to deal with Robert's plans for their future. If only she were a more emotional person, she thought wistfully. It wouldn't seem so cold-blooded then, discussing the terms of her surrender.

When she reached the porch, she noticed a car parked at the kerb, just beyond the lych-gate. It was a black saloon, long and sleek, but nothing like the racy sports car Rose Chen and her escort had arrived in a week ago. She expelled her breath rather relievedly, not really appreciating, until that moment, that she'd experienced a moment's unease. It wasn't that the sight of a strange car alarmed her, she assured herself. Because of its history, the old church occasionally attracted visitors in the summer months. It was the association with that other strange car that had startled her. And the realisation that she was not looking forward to meeting Oliver Lynch again.

Entering the church, she immediately felt the sense of peace that always invaded her consciousness whenever she did so. Perhaps she wasn't meant to be a wife at all, she reflected thoughtfully. She got so much pleasure from spiritual things; perhaps she ought to consider becoming a nun.

She was smiling to herself, thinking how horrified her father would feel at this suggestion, as she pushed open the door into the choir. It was quite dark in the church, the overcast sky leaving the pulpit in shadow. Mrs Rennie hadn't put on any of the lights; indeed, there was no sign of Mrs Rennie at all. Instead, a man was standing at the foot of the nave, gazing silently up at the altar.

Fliss's heart skipped a beat, and, although she endeavoured to calm herself, the realisation that she wasn't alone had given her quite a shock. But it wasn't just the presence of a solitary man that had startled her. It was the awareness of who that man was that had her wishing she were any place but here...

# CHAPTER FOUR

IT WAS Oliver Lynch. Even without the evidence of his superior height, she would have known it was him immediately. It was something she didn't understand; something she certainly didn't wish to consider. A kind of recognition in her bones that left her feeling weak.

Why he should have this effect on her, she had no idea. It wasn't as if she even liked the man. Their conversation on the terrace at Sutton Grange had left her with the uneasy impression that he could be totally ruthless if the occasion warranted it. And he'd had only contempt for Robert, of that she was very sure.

And now, here he was, invading the only place of sanctuary she had ever found. In a black shirt and black jeans, low-heeled black boots echoing solidly on the stone flags, he approached her, his expression mildly amused at her obvious disconcertment.

He appeared to be alone. A quick glance round the church assured her that the Chinese woman was not with him. So where was she? At the Grange? And why wasn't he driving the Ferrari today, if the car outside was his?

But all these thoughts were secondary to her own unwelcome reaction to the man himself. Everything about him—from the perverse length of his hair to the lazy sensuality of his mouth—assaulted her senses. Even the way he moved was almost sinful in its grace and sexuality, and when he tucked his thumbs into the back of his belt his appeal was frankly carnal.

'Hi,' he said, and she wondered if he had recognised her as instantly as she had recognised him. Probably not, she decided tensely. He had to be aware of the effect he had on women.

'Um—hello,' she responded, rather offhandedly, wishing she had something in her hands—a vase or a bunch of flowers, for example—to give her a reason for being there. She'd hate him to think she'd followed him.

'You're right,' he said, reaching the step that led up to the choir stalls, and resting one powerful hand on the rail. 'It is a beautiful little church. I'm glad you told me about it.'

Fliss wished she hadn't, but she took a steadying breath and moved out into the aisle. 'We like it,' she said, and for all her efforts to appear casual, she knew her voice sounded clipped. She swallowed. 'Is—Miss Chen with you? I didn't notice her car.'

'*My* car—or at least the car I've hired—is outside,' said Oliver, hopefully getting the message Fliss had been trying to convey. 'And no: Rose isn't with me. I drove down from London on my own.'

'Oh.'

Fliss absorbed this with mixed feelings. She'd heard that Robert's half-sister had found an apartment in London, that she intended to lease while she was in England. It obviously wasn't practical for her to stay in an hotel, and although they'd stayed at the Moathouse in Market Risborough for a couple of nights they'd soon left the district. Besides, Robert said staying there had just been a ploy to get them into Sutton Grange. A successful ploy, as it had turned out. People were naturally less guarded in their own home.

And now, hearing Oliver say that he'd driven down from London confirmed that they were obviously still together. And why not? She was probably his meal ticket, for heaven's sake. Whatever her father said, she believed Oliver Lynch was not just along for the ride.

'That's the house where you live, next door,' he remarked, and Fliss was so relieved he hadn't said anything controversial that she nodded.

'The vicarage,' she agreed, smoothing her damp palms over the seams of her trousers. 'It's old, too; though not as old as the church,' she conceded.

'And your father's the vicar of Sutton Magna?'

'Of Sutton Magna, Sherborne and Eryholme, actually,' Fliss said, with an involuntary smile. 'It sounds grand, but it isn't really. Sutton Magna has the largest population.'

Oliver smiled, too, his thin lips parting over teeth as attractive as the rest of him. The smile—a genuine one this time—gave his lean features an irresistible charm and personality, and Fliss's stomach quivered in involuntary response.

'I suppose you spend a lot of time here,' he said, and for a moment she was too dazed to understand what he meant. 'In the church,' he prompted, by way of an explanation. 'I gather you act as your father's deputy, as well as his secretary.'

Fliss wondered where he'd *gathered* that. Not from Robert, she was sure. Her fiancé hadn't exchanged a civil word with the American, and she doubted she was a topic of conversation when Oliver and his mistress spoke together. If they did any speaking, she appended cattily...

'Well, my mother's dead,' she told him reluctantly, bending to pluck a wilting bloom from the display of chrysanthemums that stood at the foot of the pulpit steps. 'She died while I was at university.'

'So you came home to look after your father,' said Oliver, making no attempt to get out of her way. If she wanted to move into the body of the church, she would have to get past him. And with one foot propped on the step he was a formidable obstruction.

'Er—well, he took my mother's death rather badly,' Fliss continued now, as much to keep their conversation on a fairly impersonal footing as to satisfy his curiosity. 'She—she was quite young, you see, and a clergyman needs a wife.'

Oliver frowned, his dark brows drawing together above those pale, penetrating eyes. 'So what will he do when you marry Hastings?' he asked, and Fliss's hopes of avoiding talking about her fiancé died a sudden death.

'As Robert and I will be living in the village after we're married, it shouldn't be a problem,' she declared, refusing to be any more specific than that. The fact that the Reverend Matthew Hayton had any number of village women all eager to assist him was not Oliver Lynch's business. Nor that a certain widow from Eryholme was only waiting to be asked.

Oliver's eyes narrowed. 'I got the feeling Hastings isn't too generous with your time,' he remarked casually, tipping his boot forward on to the toe, and then backward on to the heel. 'Or is that only with other men? Men who might create a problem?'

Fliss sucked in a breath. 'I don't know what you mean,' she said quickly, deciding this uneasy conversation had gone on long enough. She stepped forward. 'If you'll excuse me, I'll go and see if Mrs Rennie is in the baptistry.'

Oliver didn't move. 'She's not.'

Fliss swallowed again. 'How do you know?'

His mouth turned down, and he glanced about him. 'Because there's no one else here,' he said levelly. 'I guess she's forgotten your appointment—if you had one.'

Fliss's nostrils flared. 'Mrs Rennie asked me to help her with the flowers,' she declared, not altogether truthfully. In actual fact, she had offered to help Mrs Rennie. But, judging by the vases that were decorating every niche and table, she'd arrived a little too late.

Oliver withdrew his foot from the step and straightened. 'Well, it looks as if the old lady's been and gone,' he remarked drily, and, although Fliss had been thinking much the same thing, she bridled.

'How do you know Mrs Rennie is an old lady?' she argued, using her position on the step above him to give her some advantage. But Oliver only grinned.

'Because it was a safe bet that you wouldn't offer to help someone of your own age,' he responded. He held out his hand. 'Come on. Why don't you give me a conducted tour?'

'I—I don't have time——' Fliss ignored his hand, and edged awkwardly past him.

'No?' Oliver regarded her cynically. 'Not even the time you expected to spend with—what was that name? Mrs Rennie? Oh, Fliss, what would your father say if he could hear you tell such lies?'

Fliss halted, realising she had to put a stop to this here and now. It was obvious he enjoyed baiting her, but she didn't enjoy it. And nor did she like being made fun of just because his girlfriend wasn't around to entertain him.

'I'm sure you're perfectly capable of looking round the church on your own,' she said tersely, tilting her head. 'And just because the woman you live with has some tenuous connection with my fiancé's family, don't imagine that gives you an automatic right to the same privileges. I don't know what you're doing here, Mr Lynch, and I don't want to know. We—we've got nothing in common, and I'd prefer it if you understood that at the start.'

'Whoa!' Oliver held up a hand in mock defence. 'Did I say I expected any privileges?'

'No.' Fliss licked her lips, uneasily aware that her attempt at being condescending hadn't quite come off. 'But you can't deny that you're here, and that you expect me to be civil to you.'

'Civil!' Oliver's lips twitched, and she had the distinct impression he was laughing at her. And why not, she thought dourly. She was behaving like the irate heroine of some Victorian novel.

Sighing, she made a dismissive gesture. 'I—well, I don't know how people do things where you come from, but here we're more——' she groped for a suitable adjective '—conservative.'

'I guess.' He inclined his head. 'But I wonder where you think I do come from. You're acting as if I've got horns and a tail. What's wrong with being friendly? I'm not suggesting we have sex on the altar!'

Fliss gasped, and, as if realising he had gone too far, he uttered an impatient oath. 'I'm sorry,' he said roughly and, curiously, she knew he meant it. 'I'm not usually so graceless. You must bring out the worst in me.'

'Must I?'

Fliss's response was barely audible. She knew her chest was rising and falling, so she must be breathing, yet there didn't seem to be any air in her lungs suddenly. As he spoke, he had stepped in front of her, and now his shadow cast her into shade. But his eyes were still as vivid, grey and arresting in the pale fluted light.

He took a breath and the air he expelled stirred the tendrils of hair that clung to her damp forehead. 'Are you afraid of me, Fliss?' he asked suddenly, and her throat constricted. She knew she had never been aware of anyone as she was aware of him at that moment, and the fact that he had so accurately diagnosed her reaction was frightening.

But, 'No,' she managed swiftly, even though it hurt to say anything. Her saliva glands appeared to have stopped working, and her tongue felt swollen as it clung to the roof of her mouth.

'No?' he countered, and his mouth compressed. 'But you're not happy with me, are you?'

'I hardly know you, Mr Lynch,' she protested, wishing Mrs Rennie would appear and end this unnerving encounter. 'Um—if you don't mind, I've got to be getting back. My father will be waiting for his tea.'

'Oliver,' he said, not moving, and she frowned. 'My name's Oliver,' he repeated, as if she didn't already know it. 'The least you can do is use it, if I'm going to call you Fliss.'

'I didn't ask you to call me Fliss,' she exclaimed, and his brows arched in rueful acknowledgement.

'No,' he conceded. 'But, where I come from,' and he used the qualification deliberately, she was sure, 'we're not so formal. We even show kindness to strangers, believe it or not. We don't accuse them of—presumption, or pitch them out of our churches.'

'I never——'

Fliss broke off as the hot colour invaded her cheeks, and she wished the floor would just open up and swallow her. Everything he'd said was justified, and, while it was true that Robert wouldn't approve of this meeting, she had no good reason for behaving so churlishly.

Except her unwelcome reaction to him . . .

'OK.'

With a resigned gesture he stepped away from her, clearly taking her involuntary protest as her final word. She was free to go now, in whatever direction she liked, while he just stood there watching her with impassive guarded features.

'I——' Now it was Fliss's turn to feel rejected. 'I'm— sorry if you think we're rude.'

'We?' One dark brow arched. 'From where I'm standing there is no "we". Just you—*Miss* Hayton. There is no one else.'

Fliss hesitated. 'I've said I'm sorry.'

'Yes, so you have.' But his tone was sardonic. 'Forgive me if I don't believe you mean it.'

She pressed her lips together. 'Why did you come here, Mr Lynch?'

'Because I felt like it.' He moved his broad shoulders indifferently. 'Is that good enough for you?'

Fliss sighed, uneasily aware that their positions had been reversed. 'Because you felt like it?' she echoed.

'Right.' He ran a hand into the open collar of his shirt and massaged the muscles of his neck. 'I was at a loose end, and I felt like getting out of town. As simple as that.'

She shook her head. 'And—what will you do when you leave here? Drive back to town again?'

'Could be.'

'You're not going to the Grange?'

'No.'

She caught her lower lip between her teeth, realising that what she was about to say could be misconstrued, but saying it anyway. 'Then would you like to come and have tea with—with my father and me. It's nothing special, you understand,' she hurried on awkwardly. 'Just sandwiches and some cakes, and Mrs Neil—my father's housekeeper, that is—may have baked some scones.'

There was complete silence after she had issued her invitation. Oliver's eyes had narrowed, but his thick lashes already veiled what little expression she could read there.

Then, 'Tea?' he said harshly. 'Are you serious?'

Fliss nodded. 'Why not?'

'Why not?' Oliver's jaw sagged. 'Hell—five minutes ago you were treating me like——' He bit back the word he had been going to use and amended it to, 'dirt.' He paused. 'What changed your mind?'

Fliss shrugged, half wishing she had not been so reckless. 'Er—you did,' she admitted, after a moment. 'I think perhaps I was a little hasty. I'm sure—Rob—wouldn't want me to be inhospitable.' She lifted her head. 'Well? Would you like to join us?'

Oliver regarded her wryly. 'Let's get one thing straight, shall we?' he said. 'I don't think—Rob—would care if you spat in my eye!' He tucked his hands beneath his arms and his eyes gleamed devilishly. 'But on that understanding, I'd be happy to accept.'

Fliss glanced back towards the vestry, trying not to think how Robert would react when he found out what she'd done. 'We'll go this way,' she said, forcing herself to go ahead of him. But she was intensely aware of his eyes on her back as she hurriedly led the way out of the church.

The air outside was still muggy, but to Fliss it felt infinitely less charged than the atmosphere inside had done. But that was just her overloaded imagination, she thought impatiently. And the fact that in the churchyard Oliver didn't seem so threatening.

'These graves look pretty old,' he remarked, gesturing towards the gnarled stones whose engraved inscriptions were barely readable, and Fliss was relieved to have something positive to say.

'They are,' she said. 'Not so many people are buried these days, and the few new graves there are are over at the other side of the church. Some of these stones date back to the seventeenth century. There are even a few of the plague victims, though most of them were buried in a mass grave under the village green.'

Oliver shook his head. 'Plague victims,' he said ruefully. 'I guess we didn't have so many of them back home. The epidemic—that was in the seventeenth century, wasn't it? Just before the Great Fire that wiped out half of London.'

Fliss was surprised. 'Are you interested in English history?'

'I was.' Oliver shrugged. 'When I was studying law, we covered various aspects of the British legal system, and I guess I got hooked. Some of our laws were founded here, and it helped to understand why they were made.'

Fliss gazed at him. 'You're a lawyer?'

Oliver's mouth turned down. 'Not any more.'

'What does that mean?'

'It means I dropped out,' he said flatly, going ahead to open the gate that led into the vicarage garden. 'I guess we have something in common after all.'

Fliss's father met them on the flagged terrace that ran along the back of the house. Evidently he had abandoned his sermon for the time being, and was presently seated in a canvas chair, examining the manuscript of the article he was writing for an historical journal. He looked up in surprise when he saw his daughter crossing the lawn towards him accompanied by a strange man. Putting his papers aside, he rose to his feet, with a look of not unpleased speculation on his face.

Fliss, who was still smarting from Oliver's latest mocking comment, had some difficulty in keeping the rancour out of her voice. 'Um—this is—Mr Lynch, Dad,' she said offhandedly. 'You remember, he accompanied Robert's half-sister from Hong Kong. He was—visiting—the church, so I've invited him to tea. I—Mr Lynch, this is my father, Reverend Matthew Hayton.'

'How do you do, sir?' said Oliver politely, as the older man held out his hand. 'I hope I'm not intruding.'

'Not at all.' Fliss's father was clearly impressed by the American's courtesy. 'We don't get a lot of strangers in Sutton Magna. It's a bit of a backwater, Mr Lynch, but I must confess, I like it.'

'So do I,' answered Oliver at once, as Fliss started across the terrace, to tell Mrs Neil they had a visitor. 'You're very lucky to live in such beautiful surroundings.'

'I think so,' agreed the Reverend, gesturing the other man to a seat. 'Did I understand Felicity to say you live in Hong Kong, Mr Lynch? That must be very different from here.'

'It is. And I wish you'd call me Oliver,' he replied disarmingly. 'Fliss—Felicity—was just showing me the

graves in the churchyard. I guess the age of the head-
stones is some indication of the village's permanence.'

Fliss's jaw clenched as she went through the french
windows. Had she told Oliver Lynch that her father was
an amateur historian, he couldn't have said anything
more likely to attract the Reverend's interest. And obviously her father was prepared to accept their guest at
face value. She scowled. The trouble was, her father
always saw the best in everyone. She wondered irritably
why she couldn't do the same.

By the time she came back carrying the tray herself,
with Mrs Neil coming along behind with the teapot, the
two men were comfortably absorbed in a discussion of
the relative merits of land rights, and what evidence there
was that large estates benefited from continual
ownership.

'I realise that we're talking about vastly different areas
of tenure,' her father was saying earnestly. 'Naturally,
untended open spaces need good land management, or
the kind of erosion you spoke of can take place.' He cast
an absent glance up at Fliss, as she set the tray on the
wicker table beside him, and then continued, undeterred, 'But is it fair that one family or one concern
should own thousands of acres of our countryside, when,
if it was split into smaller holdings or farms, we might
not get the drift of young people into the cities in search
of employment?'

'I'm not sure the two things are mutually compatible,'
said Oliver, getting to his feet and waiting for Fliss to
sit down before resuming his own seat. 'Back home, kids
seek the city life regardless. They're not interested in
working fourteen-hour days just so they can say a place
is their own. Hell, small towns bore them!' He grimaced. 'Excuse me. But I've seen too many kids in the
courtroom who thought living in the city was the
American dream!'

'In the courtroom?' exclaimed Fliss's father with interest, and then, realising he was ignoring his daughter, he made an apologetic gesture. 'You must forgive me, my dear, but it's so rarely that I find someone with whom I can share my views. Did you know Oliver studied law at Harvard? And he knows all about our feudal system and the outdated laws it established.'

'Not all,' said Oliver modestly, but Fliss couldn't help resenting the way he had beguiled her father. It was years since she had seen the older man look so animated about anyone, and it took a great deal of self-control not to demonstrate her feelings.

Mrs Neil set the teapot on the table, and stood back to admire her handiwork. Sandwiches, which were slightly more substantial than they should be; a sponge cake Fliss had made, which she was sure would be heavy as lead; and the famous fruit scones, a favourite at village fêtes—whose presence could usually ensure a complimentary response from their guests.

'It all looks most delicious, Mrs Neil,' Matthew Hayton declared, as he always did, and the elderly housekeeper beamed.

'There's more tea, if you want it, Vicar,' she said, giving Oliver an inquisitive stare. 'You'll come and get it, won't you, Fliss? It'll save my old legs a journey.'

'Of course.'

Fliss spoke quietly enough, but Mrs Neil had drawn attention to her once again. Not that she thought Oliver had ever quite forgotten her, but the housekeeper's words had given him the excuse to taunt her with his smile.

Mrs Neil withdrew, and Fliss realised it was up to her to pour the tea. It was what she did every afternoon, after all, but today she could have done without the responsibility. She was sure her hands were shaking; sure Oliver Lynch knew exactly how she felt. It was infuriating that he should look so at home here. But, like a chameleon, he adapted himself to any situation.

'You said—back home?' her father remarked, and she was so relieved that he had spoken she could have hugged him. She actually sensed the moment when Oliver's clear, penetrating eyes were removed from the downward curve of her cheek, and she hurried to attend to the cups while his interest was elsewhere.

'I assume you mean back home in the United States,' the older man prompted, and although Fliss told herself she wasn't interested, she couldn't help listening for his answer.

'Yes. Virginia,' replied Oliver at once, relaxed and disturbingly familiar in the chair beside hers. With one ankle propped across his knee, and one lean, brown-fingered hand resting on it, he should have presented no problem to her at all. But the rolled-back cuffs of his shirt meant his muscled forearm was close to her sleeve, and one powerful thigh was uncomfortably near her leg.

It was a hairy forearm, she noticed uneasily, as she splashed hot tea into the cups. A slim watch, on a leather strap made a distinctive band across his wrist, and there was that scar that started below his elbow and disappeared under his sleeve. She wondered when he had acquired that, and whether she'd really like to know.

'Virginia,' echoed her father, as Fliss forced herself to concentrate on what she was doing and nothing else. 'Of course, you'll know it was named after our first Queen Elizabeth, the "virgin" queen, as she was known. What part of the state do you come from?'

'The south-west,' replied Oliver easily, apparently willing to satisfy her father's curiosity. 'A small town called Maple Falls. Do you know it?'

'I'm afraid not.' Matthew Hayton turned to take the tea his daughter offered him. 'Apart from the capital—Richmond, isn't it?—and Chesapeake Bay, I know very little about the area. I've never been to the United States, you see. I'm just an armchair traveller.'

'You must try it some time,' said Oliver, and, although Fliss had managed to avoid his eyes up till now, the necessity of asking how he liked his tea brought his gaze into conflict with hers again. 'You too—Felicity,' he added, after accepting milk but no sugar. Then, knowing it would annoy her, 'Perhaps you could persuade Robert to take you to the States for your honeymoon.'

'I think not,' said Fliss stiffly, aware that her father was watching them now, and compelled to be polite.

'No, I think Rob's more likely to choose Bermuda,' put in the Reverend with a smile. 'I understand it has some good golfcourses, and my future son-in-law is quite a fanatic.'

'Dad!'

Fliss was flushed, but Oliver only said, 'Really?' and let the older man expand.

'My goodness, yes,' exclaimed her father cheerfully. 'I've often said Rob's infinitely more at home on the golfcourse than he is in the boardroom. I don't know what will happen to Hastings' if he's in the chair. Without his father's brilliance, I fear the company may fold.'

'Do you?'

Oliver sounded intrigued, and Fliss hurriedly pushed the sandwiches in her father's direction, hoping his interest in the food might distract him from discussing Robert's business. But Matthew Hayton was so used to speaking to people who had no ulterior motives that it didn't occur to him to think Oliver Lynch might have motives of his own.

'I'm afraid so.' The older man nodded now, accepting a sandwich, but studying it before he took a bite. 'I dare say your—fiancée—knows all about the problems they're facing.'

'Rose Chen is not my fiancée,' said Oliver flatly, as Fliss cast an unwary glance towards him. 'But, you're right, the company is facing certain—difficulties. I don't suppose—Rob—has mentioned anything about it to you.'

'Good heavens, no.' The Reverend laughed. 'I doubt Rob knows one end of a balance sheet from the other.' He frowned. 'It may be that your—that *Miss Chen's* intervention could be a blessing in disguise. I understand she has been involved in the Hong Kong end of the business for some time.'

'Yes.' Oliver sounded thoughtful. 'So you don't think your daughter's fiancé enjoyed his father's confidence?'

'Well, if he did, he hid it very well,' declared her father ruefully, and Fliss, who had been making a concerted effort to enjoy her tea, banged the cup into the saucer with unnecessary force.

'If you'll excuse me,' she said, bestowing a less than approving look on both of them, and, snatching up the teapot, she marched into the house.

# CHAPTER FIVE

MRS NEIL had gone, she saw at once, leaving the casserole she had prepared for supper waiting to be put in the oven. Another pot of tea was sheltering under a padded cosy, just in case it was needed. But Fliss didn't bother to uncover it. Instead, she carried the empty pot over to the sink and dropped the used teabags into the waste bin. She needed a few minutes to herself, she thought wryly. It wasn't just the humidity that was making her feel so limp.

She was letting water from the cold tap cool her wrists when she sensed she was no longer alone. She didn't quite know how she knew, but she felt as if the air in the room had quickened. When she glanced round and saw him, she couldn't say she was altogether surprised. But that didn't make his appearance any more welcome, and her heart raced accordingly.

Moistening her lips, keeping her hands under the cool water, she looked at him over her shoulder. 'Yes?'

'I've brought the tray,' Oliver said, and she realised her eyes had never left his face.

'Oh—thanks,' she offered lamely, forcing her attention back to the sink. 'Just put it on the table, would you?'

She heard the thunk as the tray was set on the scrubbed pine of the kitchen table, and then strained her ears to hear the sound of his departure. He wouldn't stay, she assured herself. Not when her father knew where she was. And what excuse could he give for talking to her, when Matthew Hayton was so much enjoying their conversation?

'I like your father,' he said suddenly, and she realised
his deck shoes had made no sound on the tiled floor.
He was standing beside her now, to one side of the porcelain sink. She'd been so intent on wishing him gone,
she'd missed the sound of his approach.

'So do I,' she managed awkwardly now, turning off
the tap, and reaching for a paper towel to dry her hands.
Then, reluctantly, 'I—er—I hope you won't take what
he says too—too literally. Robert isn't really as useless
as my father likes to make out.'

Oliver's mouth twisted. 'I'm not into telling tales,' he
remarked, lodging his hips against the drainer and regarding her with steady eyes. 'Besides, I'd like to come
here again. I wouldn't want to screw up my welcome.'

Fliss stared at him. 'Why would you want to come
here again?' she protested, not a little disturbed by his
answer.

Oliver's eyes dropped to her mouth. 'Why do you
think?' he asked, that blatant gaze searing her lips like
a fire. Dear God, she thought, it was as if he'd touched
her. His silvery eyes were as sensual as the disturbing
curve of his mouth.

'I think——' Her own mouth dried, and with a concerted effort she started again. 'I think you ought to go,
Mr Lynch. I don't know what you want with us, but I
know you're wasting your time.'

'Am I?' He moved then, fluidly and sensuously,
stretching out his hand and linking his fingers loosely
about her wrist. It seemed to happen in slow motion,
and she should have had the chance to avoid him. But
this whole affair had an unreal quality that left her feeling
weak. 'What if I say I don't think so?'

A *frisson* of alarm slid down Fliss's spine. 'You're—
impertinent, Mr Lynch,' she said, forcing herself not to
panic. 'I suggest you let me go before my father comes
to find us.'

'Oh, I don't think he'll do that.' Oliver sounded absurdly confident, lifting her wrist to his mouth and tracing the network of veins on the inner side with his tongue. He licked his lips then, as if the taste of her met with his approval. 'When I left him, he was dozing. If I didn't know better I'd have suspected you'd spiked his tea.'

Fliss gasped. 'You didn't——'

'No, I didn't.' Oliver sounded mildly put out. 'For God's sake, what do you take me for? I'm not your enemy, Fliss. Though I suspect you wish I were.'

'I don't know what you mean.' Fliss made a not very dignified effort to free herself, which met with no success. Panting, she exclaimed, 'You're not my friend, Mr Lynch. I don't even like you. And I don't think you care about anyone but yourself.'

Oliver's expression didn't change, but his response was vaguely wounded. 'So, what have I done to deserve an attack like that? I thought we were making some progress earlier on.'

Fliss blinked. 'Progress?' She shook her head. 'Progress towards what?'

'Towards being friends, of course,' he answered softly, his gaze straying from the downy sweep of her cheek to the unbuttoned neckline of her shirt. 'I want us to be friends, Fliss.' His mouth curled. 'I want us to be more than that, but it will do for a start.'

Fliss felt as if she was choking. And, although she was sure he couldn't see anything beyond the sun-tinted column of her throat, the skin in the V darkened anyway. Between her breasts, a tiny trickle of perspiration dampened her bra, and deep down in her stomach that uneasy torment stirred.

'I don't want to be your friend,' she said unsteadily, wishing, for the first time, that Robert would come and interrupt this illicit confrontation. Oliver Lynch was frightening her—or was she frightening herself?

'What do you want?' he asked, and now his free hand came to stroke along the curve of her cheek. His thumb brushed the slightly parted corner of her mouth, and although she snapped her lips together instantly she could still taste the saltiness of his skin.

'Nothing,' she gulped, but she knew he was hardly paying attention to her words. His fingertips had invaded the silky curtain of her hair, drawing it forward against her cheek, and rubbing it against her skin.

'You're beautiful,' he said, his hand finding the nape of her neck now and drawing her insistently towards him. 'Don't tell me you don't want to know that. Because you know what?' He tilted her face up to his. 'I'm not going to believe that either.'

Fliss knew she should be struggling, knew she should be using any means within her power to get away from him. If she didn't do something soon he was going to kiss her, and then how disgusted with herself she would feel, knowing she could have stopped him. Not to mention the fact that she was betraying Robert by just standing here. Just letting Oliver Lynch touch her wrist and her lips and her hair. Dear God, she was practically condoning his behaviour. Why didn't she slap his arrogant face or bury her fist in his flat stomach? She had the feeling he wouldn't stop her. So what was she waiting for?

'Please,' she said, and hearing the pleading note in her voice she despised herself anew, 'if I've given you the wrong impression, if you think I'm—well, I'm sorry. But—I am—engaged to Robert.'

'I know.' He conceded her words without concession, his breath warm against her flushed cheeks. 'So why do you look so—innocent? If you are Hastings'—lover—why do you act as if you're untouched?'

'I don't. I'm not——' Fliss was panicking, and she knew it. But she could feel his legs against hers now, and the caressing fingers at her nape were forcing her upper body into intimate contact with his. Already her breasts, taut and knotted with emotions she didn't even want to recognise, were nudging the dark fabric of his shirt. Did he know? Could he feel their raw excitement? Did he realise what he was doing to her? Oh, God, of course he did. He knew exactly what he was doing.

'Let's find out,' he murmured huskily, releasing her wrist to slide both hands into the sun-streaked tumble of her hair. With infinite patience, he positioned her face, and then, with equal deliberation, he lowered his mouth to hers.

Fliss's head swam at the first touch of his lips. His kiss was so different from Robert's, light, and not at all intrusive, tasting her gently, yet inciting her response. He didn't constrain her, or force her, but she was intensely conscious of his power. He held her very loosely, yet very purposefully, brushing her mouth insistently and biting softly at her lips.

Fliss's legs turned to jelly. Her bones felt soft, malleable, barely capable of supporting her weight. She couldn't have moved away to save her life, and instead she found herself swaying against him, inviting him to touch her, luxuriating in the way her breasts flattened against his chest. She leant into him shamelessly, allowing the sinful embrace to continue, almost mindless with delight.

He parted his legs so that when his hands moved down her back to her hips she was automatically drawn between them. His strong fingers caressed her spine and the rounded curve of her bottom, moulding her against him, so that she could feel every intimate angle of his body. Allowing her to feel his hard arousal, letting her sense the awareness of danger that was so barely leashed.

But before her dazed mind could absorb that thought and act on it, Oliver deepened the kiss, his mouth settling ever more surely over hers. And because she was hot and breathless, and desperate for air, her lips parted automatically, and his tongue found no opposition to its entry. On the contrary, she welcomed its muscled invasion with an eager urgency, and a low moan rose in her throat as he ravaged her yielding mouth.

Heat spread like a raging fire along her veins. Its core was in the passionate melding of their lips. Oliver's kiss seduced her and drugged her, made her a willing prisoner to his demands. She couldn't think, she couldn't act, she could only feel. And, in that feeling, react to the wildly erotic madness he was inspiring.

She clutched at him urgently, finding the opened collar of his shirt and the hair-roughened skin beneath. Skin that was hot and male, and responsive to her desires. But—unfamiliar. This was not Robert—had she ever thought it was? This man was a stranger to her. And she was giving him freedoms she had never allowed her fiancé.

And, as this thought brought her brain into reluctant action, horror began to take the place of bemusement. What was she doing? she asked herself, appalled at the shameless way she had been responding to his touch. What was she thinking of, allowing the man to *use* her? The swollen thrust of Oliver's sex against her stomach was not exciting any more, it was disgusting. How could she have permitted such unbridled lust to possess her? It wasn't possible; it wasn't like her. She wasn't a wanton; she was a lady. And ladies didn't pant and moan like a cross-bred bitch in heat.

Tearing her mouth from his, she spread her palms against his chest and pushed. And, perhaps because Oliver had been as dazed by his emotions as she had until that moment, his hands dropped unresistingly to his thighs. She was free, and with a jerky backward movement she put some space between them, grasping the table behind her for some badly needed support.

'I—think you'd better go,' she said tensely, realising how inadequate words were at a time like this. Watching him, *hating* him, despising him for what he had done to her, she just wanted him to leave. She wanted him out of her sight, before she gave in to the temptation to attack him physically. She wanted to scratch his eyes out, for making her feel so cheap.

'If that's what you want,' he said at last, his lids drooping, his eyes still heavy with the aftermath of their lovemaking. If she hadn't known better she'd have said he looked as shocked as she was, his harsh features hollowed, deep lines engraved beside his mouth.

'Of course it's what I want,' she told him fiercely, holding on to her composure with some difficulty. 'If you remember, it's what I asked you to do before— before——'

'Before I kissed you?' he prompted, brows arching in a strangely self-deprecatory gesture, and Fliss's mouth compressed.

'Before you ruined a perfectly good afternoon,' she retorted, ignoring the taunting voice inside her that hinted at another interpretation. 'What do you expect me to say, Mr Lynch? I think you're absolutely despicable. I invited you here in good faith, and this is how you've repaid me.' She hesitated a moment, and then added bitterly, 'Aren't you ashamed?'

Oliver smoothed his palms along his thighs before straightening, and although Fliss's instinctive reaction was to recoil from him, she stood her ground. Nevertheless, she couldn't meet his eyes, and she had to forcibly restrain herself from looking at his trousers.

'Do you want to tell me what I'm supposed to be ashamed of?' he suggested at last, and although his tone was mild there was an underlying note of warning. Evidently, like her, his brain was functioning again, and, contrary to her hopes, he didn't regret a thing.

'For—for abusing my father's hospitality,' she declared primly, finding it difficult to put her own outrage into words. Would she have felt as outraged if he hadn't

threatened the image she had always kept of herself?
Was it because he had breached her defences that she
felt so resentful now?

But no. She calmed her rising panic with a fervent
effort. It wasn't just resentment she was feeling, but in-
dignation too. On Robert's behalf. What could you say
to a man who thought nothing of making love to another
man's fiancée? How could you get him to feel shame,
when it wasn't in his vocabulary?

And, as he had still made no response, she went on
doggedly, 'How do you think he—my father—would feel
if he knew what you'd been doing? In spite of his doubts
about Robert's competence in the boardroom, he does
respect him, you know.'

'Does he?'

Oliver was laconic, and Fliss felt even more aggrieved. If only she didn't feel so guilty herself, she
thought frustratedly. If only she'd repulsed him before
things had gone so far.

But, 'Yes, he does,' she averred now, lifting a hand
and pushing back the heavy weight of her hair. It was
damp close to her scalp, the tendrils moist and clinging.
He had done that to her, she thought. She'd never got
so hot and bothered with Robert.

'Well, good for him,' drawled Oliver, his eyes following her every move. 'Forgive me, but I got a different impression.'

'Well, you would,' said Fliss, feeling suddenly weary.
'Anyway—that doesn't alter the fact that I want you to
go. Now.'

'OK.' Oliver inclined his head. 'Never let it be said
that I refused a lady.' He paused, his eyes mocking her.
'Anything.'

'But why would you go there, of all places?' demanded
Rose Chen angrily. 'For God's sake, Lee, are you trying
to make a fool of me?'

Oliver's grey eyes narrowed. 'Why would my going to Sutton Magna have any effect on you?' he inquired evenly. 'My life is my own, Rose. I may have agreed to come to England, but I never agreed that you should have some divine right to organise my movements. I wanted out of the city, and Sutton Magna seemed as good a place as any.' His brows arched. 'Besides, I'd have thought you'd be interested to hear what other people have to say about your brother.'

'My *half*-brother,' corrected Rose Chen tersely, flinging herself into one of the comfortable armchairs in the living-room of the penthouse apartment she had leased in Knightsbridge. 'And why should I be interested in what some old priest thinks of Robert? I know what he is. He's an ass. He doesn't know the first thing about the company.'

'Doesn't he?' Oliver adjusted his position against the mantel, endeavouring not to sound too interested. 'What makes you say that?'

'Oh—you know!' Rose Chen sounded exasperated. 'You've sat in on the meetings. As far as he's concerned, Jay-Jay was running a small but fairly profitable business in fine arts. He specialised in jade and precious metals, with a fairly lucrative sideline in oriental porcelain. He used the handful of shops he owned to distribute the merchandise, and everyone thought he was a respectable entrepreneur.'

Oliver tensed. 'And he wasn't?'

Rose Chen looked up at him critically. 'Oh, yes. He was,' she said, lifting one hand and examining her finger nails. 'Very respectable, as it happens.' Her eyes narrowed now. 'Didn't you think so?'

Oliver let his breath out on a careful sigh. 'I don't think I have an opinion, one way or the other,' he replied, aware that he had been in danger of appearing too interested. 'It's nothing to do with me, is it?' He sauntered across the room to the tray of drinks residing on a side table. Then, indicating the various bottles and glasses, 'D'you want something?'

Rose Chen hesitated. 'Do you think I'm a fool, Lee?' she asked, crossing one slender leg over the other, and for a moment Oliver felt the cold draught of exposure invading his spine.

'A fool?' he echoed, playing for time, and to his relief Rose Chen transferred her gaze to her fingernails again.

'Yes, a fool,' she said, but there was no rancour in her voice now. 'I'm sure Robert Hastings does. But that's because he doesn't know me.' She snorted. 'God help him, he didn't even know his own father!' She shook her head. 'Can you believe that? Jay-Jay didn't even tell his son what he was doing.'

Oliver raised the glass of Scotch he had poured himself to his lips. 'Didn't he?' he asked casually. 'Well, I've heard that's not uncommon in a society that sends its kids to private school as soon as they're old enough to tie their own bootlaces.'

'Public school,' amended Rose Chen automatically. 'Robert went to public school, Lee. That's what they call it here. A pretty famous one, I believe. Jay-Jay used to talk about the education he'd given his son.' She grimaced. 'Of course, I didn't know he was talking about my own half-brother at that time.'

Oliver hesitated. 'And how does that make you feel? Now, I mean? Do you resent the fact that—that your father didn't treat you as he treated his son?'

Rose Chen sighed. 'Sometimes.'

Oliver inclined his head. 'But it seems he did trust you more than he did Robert,' he ventured, and Rose Chen gave him another speculative look.

'What do you mean by that?'

Oliver gave an inward groan. 'You've just said that Robert didn't know his father,' he defended himself tersely, and expelled a relieved breath when Rose Chen's shoulders sagged.

'Oh, yes,' she said ruefully. 'I'm sorry. I know I must sound paranoid to you, but honestly, it's hell when you don't even know who your friends are.'

'Well...' Oliver chose his words with care. 'I'd have thought you could confide in the Hastingses. After all, it's in their best interests to co-operate, isn't it?'

Rose Chen's expression was unreadable, and Oliver reflected that the term 'inscrutable oriental' was not as dramatic as some people might think.

'You don't understand,' she said finally.

'Then explain it to me.'

'I can't.'

Oliver shrugged. 'OK.' Hiding his own disappointment under a veil of indifference, he indicated the drinks again. 'Are you sure I can't offer you something? A glass of wine? Sherry?'

Rose Chen shook her head. 'Nothing,' she said, tipping her head back against the dark upholstery. Then, tilting her gaze towards him again, she said softly, 'Can I trust you, Lee? Can I really trust you?'

'Do you doubt it?' responded Oliver obliquely, not liking the brief surge of contempt he felt for his own position. But then, common sense, and the bleak knowledge of what James Hastings—and perhaps Rose Chen too—had really been doing overrode any finer feelings he might have entertained. 'Have I ever given you a reason not to?'

'N—o.' Rose Chen conceded the word slowly. 'Except I don't like you speaking to anyone behind my back, in my best interests or otherwise.'

'The Haytons,' said Oliver flatly. 'Rose——'

'You saw Felicity Hayton, too?' Rose Chen abandoned her reclining position and came upright in her seat. 'You didn't tell me that.'

Oliver expelled his breath wearily. 'Yes, I did——'

'No, you didn't.' Rose was very certain about that. 'You gave me to understand that you met Father Hayton in the churchyard. You didn't say a thing about his daughter.'

'He's a *Reverend*,' Oliver corrected her now, using the ploy to give him time to think. 'And I don't believe I said how I met him. As a matter of fact, it was Fli—Felicity—I met while I was looking round the church. She recognised me——'

'Of course.' Scornfully.

'—and she invited me to tea with herself and her father. End of explanation.'

'As simple as that.'

'As simple as that,' agreed Oliver shortly, cursing himself for creating the distraction. He wasn't certain, of course, but it had seemed that Rose Chen had been on the verge of confiding in him. Now she was more concerned with his relationship with Fliss. And although Oliver knew she had some reason for her suspicions, she didn't know that.

She *mustn't* know that, he reminded himself grimly. Whatever kind of fool he had made of himself with Fliss Hayton, Rose Chen must never find out. Not if he hoped to continue with his investigation. And, after all, that was the only reason he was here...

'So...' Rose Chen regarded him with vaguely hostile eyes now. 'What do you think of her? The Hayton woman, I mean. I noticed you made a beeline for her that first day we went to Sutton Grange.' She uttered a short laugh. 'Funny, I didn't think she was your type.'

'She's not.' Oliver's response was harsher than he'd intended, but frustration was a hard task-master. 'Dammit, Rose, can't I speak to another woman without you accusing me of God knows what?'

Amazingly, his bitterness achieved what logic hadn't. Now it was Rose Chen's turn to look a little shamefaced, and she pushed herself up out of the chair and came towards him with little-girl ruefulness.

'I'm sorry,' she said, tucking her arm through his, and resting her head against his shoulder. 'I'm a bitch, and I know it. But, you don't know what it's like, Lee. You're the only person I can be myself with. The Hastingses—Jay-Jay's employees—they're all strangers to me. I don't even know if they trust me. But, you're different. You're my friend; my lover; my man! I don't like it when you show interest in other women. Any other women. But particularly not the woman Robert's going to marry.'

Oliver contained his impatience. 'I wasn't showing interest in her,' he lied tautly. 'For Pete's sake, Rose, we had tea with her father. How was I supposed to come on to the woman with her father breathing down my neck?'

How indeed? he chided himself mockingly, remembering that interlude in the Haytons' kitchen with a feeling akin to disbelief. Dear God, he had nearly seduced the woman in her own kitchen. Would have seduced her, too, if she hadn't belatedly come to her senses. His body still ached with the aftermath of aborted passion, and, crazy as it seemed, he could still feel the imprint of her breasts against his chest, still rise to the pressure of her thighs against his pelvis, still smell the light fragrance of her perfume mingling with the clean scent of her body...

'I know, I know,' Rose Chen was assuring him now, as he revelled in the treacherous memories of another embrace. 'I'm just a jealous cow, and I don't deserve you. But be patient with me, Lee. This isn't an easy time for me, and I guess I'm looking for trouble in the most unlikely places.'

'Trouble?' Oliver managed to sound only marginally interested. 'What trouble?'

'You don't want to know,' said Rose Chen, drawing away to run one scarlet-tipped nail down his roughening

cheek. 'You need a shave, darling. But don't worry. I
like you rough or smooth.' Her voice grew husky. 'Come
with me and I'll show you.'

# CHAPTER SIX

FLISS viewed her appearance in the long cheval glass in her bedroom with a critical eye. Dinner parties were not her ideal form of entertainment, and this particular dinner party promised to have more than its share of problems. Oliver Lynch was going to be there, for one thing, and, apart from the obvious pitfalls that portended, Robert was in no mood to be amenable.

Ever since he had learned that Oliver Lynch had had tea with his fiancée and his prospective father-in-law, he had been less than conciliatory. It was his opinion that Fliss had been far too friendly towards someone whose involvement with his family was decidedly dubious. It was bad enough, he said, having to be civil to his father's bastard. Fliss had had no right to treat the American like any ordinary guest in their house. So far as Robert was concerned, Oliver Lynch was a freeloader and a parasite, using his association with the Chinese woman to gain entry to polite society.

Polite society? Fliss chided herself now, recalling the less than polite way Oliver had taken advantage of her. And he *had* taken advantage of her, she assured herself firmly. Just because she hadn't prevented him from holding her and touching her, and treating her in a way she had never allowed any man to treat her before, was no excuse for his behaviour. He had abused her father's hospitality, as she had said, and his mockery of her accusations didn't make them any the less appropriate.

All the same, she had had a few bad moments since that encounter in the kitchen. Even before she had had to confess to Oliver's visit, she had found it incredibly difficult to put what had happened between them to the back of her mind. Not least when she was with her fiancé, she admitted unwillingly. It was virtually impossible not to feel some sense of guilt when Robert took her in his arms, and the fact that she was still holding him at arm's length was another source of shame to her.

She was confused, that was all, she told herself now. Instead of making her relationship with Robert easier, it had merely complicated the situation, making her twice as sensitive to feelings of doubt and uncertainty. She still loved Robert—of course she did—but so long as Oliver Lynch was around she was going to find it hard to dissociate herself from his treachery.

And now, there was this dinner party to contend with. After her husband's betrayal, Fliss didn't see why Mrs Hastings should want to give a dinner party for the woman who was threatening to destroy the life she had striven for all these years. If everything Robert said was to be believed, Rose Chen had quickly installed herself in the position of greatest authority in the company, and he was already complaining that she, as much as his father, was denying him the birthright he deserved.

If only she didn't have to be involved, Fliss thought wearily. She agreed with Robert: there should have been no question of who inherited the business, and his father had treated him abominably by not warning him of what he planned to do. But then, that would have meant revealing his relationship to Rose Chen sooner, and who knew what a clever lawyer might have made of James Hastings' intentions of acknowledging his illegitimate daughter. Certainly, Robert and his mother and the twins would have had a good case for compensation, without the obvious advantages that Hastings' indiscretion would have given them.

But James Hastings had been nothing if not cunning, and Fliss, who had always found him rather too smooth, was not at all surprised that he had chosen to deceive all of them. She even believed Rose Chen had been as ignorant of her real identity as the rest of them, and although she didn't like the woman she had some sympathy for her position, at least.

Which still didn't make the reasons for this dinner party any easier to understand, Fliss reflected now, giving her appearance a critical appraisal. It simply wasn't like Amanda Hastings to be so accommodating, and she was not looking forward to having to make small talk with the woman whose arrival had made such a significant dent in her own normally placid existence.

Now, thrusting the connotations of that particular thought aside, Fliss turned from side to side, viewing her appearance from every angle possible. Was the dress suitable? she wondered, for the umpteenth time. In the shop in Market Risborough it had looked a lot better than it did now, and she had the unpleasant feeling that it was not the sort of thing to wear to a social gathering at your future in-laws'. It was far too clinging, for one thing, and the V neckline which had appeared almost conservative in the boutique now seemed to expose an inordinate amount of cleavage. Who would have thought that dusky pink satin could look so—so revealing? It had loose, elbow-length sleeves, for heaven's sake, and the hem fell to well below mid-calf. It should have looked modest. Instead, it accentuated her bosom, and drew attention to the narrow waist above far too generous hips.

But time was getting on, and, deciding there was nothing she could do about it now, Fliss transferred her attention to her hair. The silky fall of sun-bleached hair had been secured in a loose knot on top of her head, and she hoped the fact that it was newly washed wouldn't cause any other mishap. Already, several golden tendrils were curling beside the gold hoops that dangled from her ears, and she could only hope that people would think they were a deliberate affectation.

She sighed as she smoothed a dusky coral gloss over her lips. She didn't really know why she was making such a fuss. It was just a dinner party, for heaven's sake. The way she was acting, anyone would think her life depended on it.

Well, perhaps it did, she conceded unsteadily as she went downstairs to greet her fiancé. This might be her last chance to convince Oliver Lynch that whatever he cared to think, she shared her fiancé's opinion of him.

All the same, she hoped Robert wouldn't cause a scene. In spite of her convictions, she had the unhappy feeling that in an exchange of words or actions the American was unlikely to flinch from using any weapons at his disposal. And, unfortunately, she herself had provided him with the perfect ammunition.

Robert was waiting in the sitting-room, enjoying a glass of sherry with her father. The two men were obviously having difficulty in finding any mutual source of discussion, and in consequence they both turned towards Fliss with evident relief.

'Hey!'

'My, my!'

The two men's reactions were reassuringly positive, but Fliss wasn't altogether happy with the look in Robert's eyes. There was a distinctly proprietorial gleam there, and she wished now she had had the guts to tell him what Oliver Lynch had done. Not that it would have made their relationship any easier, but at least it would have denied the American any chance of making a fool of him. As it was, she felt she was going out to dinner under false pretences, and accepting Robert's compliments in much the same spirit.

'You look very pretty, my dear.'

It was her father who made the first motion towards her, taking her hands in his, and surveying her as he used to do years ago when she was on her way to a friend's birthday party.

'Doesn't she, though?'

Robert's response was more personal, and when her father released her hands he drew her into an uncomfortably close embrace. Really, Fliss thought, with a faintly hysterical sense of *déjà vu*, Robert was getting decidedly possessive. Was it just his reaction to their engagement, or was he simply staking his claim? Either way, she dreaded Oliver Lynch's response if her fiancé chose to make an issue of it.

'Well—enjoy yourselves, won't you?' the Reverend adjured them now, and Fliss could tell he wasn't happy with such a blatant display of possession.

'I will,' Robert replied, apparently immune to any feelings of disapproval. 'How could I do anything else when I'm going to be with the most beautiful woman there?'

Robert's Jaguar was waiting outside, and he helped Fliss inside with evident delight. 'You do look stunning,' he added, as he came round the bonnet and got in beside her. He leaned over to find her mouth, but Fliss turned her head away.

'Lipstick,' she said hurriedly, as his kiss landed on her cheek. Then, rather breathily, 'Isn't it warm?'

'Well, I'm warm, certainly,' agreed Robert, though as his eyes moved over her again his meaning was obvious. 'Just let Lynch make any move towards you this evening. I'm just in the mood to tell him exactly where to get off.'

Fliss swallowed. 'Oh, Rob——'

'Oh, don't worry. I won't start anything,' Robert assured her impatiently, as he started the car. 'I've already promised my mother I won't cause any trouble. She knows how I feel about this dinner party, but she has some crazy idea that if we antagonise Rose Chen we might do something to upset the apple-cart.'

Fliss frowned. 'I don't understand. What could she do?'

'Well, you know she's virtually taken over the running of the company?'

'Hardly that, surely.'

'Oh, yes.' Robert was bitter. 'Just because I was never pally with the employees, she's used that to insinuate herself into everybody's good books. They all think she's the only one who knows what's going on, and no matter how I try to get a handle on things she's always there first.'

Fliss sighed. 'Are you sure you're not exaggerating, Rob? I mean, Rose Chen was a stranger to these people——'

'Don't I know it?' Robert snorted. 'Sometimes I think if Father wasn't dead I'd feel like killing him myself! He's ruined my life, do you know that, Fliss? I'm never going to amount to anything, and I've only got him to blame.'

Fliss hesitated. 'But—well, you do have other options, Rob.'

'What? What options?'

'Well, you have a fairly good degree in business studies.'

'So?'

'So—why not let—Rose Chen buy you out, if she's willing to? You could use the money to start your own business——'

'What kind of business?'

'I don't know.' Fliss was beginning to wish she'd never got involved in this. 'What do you know about?' She waited, and when he said nothing, she added awkwardly, 'You could always start your own import and export company. Maybe you could keep a couple of the shops——'

'I'm not a shop-keeper, Fliss.' Robert sounded insulted now. 'For God's sake, surely you can see I'm going to have to deal with Rose Chen, whether I like it or not?'

'And—and that's what this dinner party is all about?'

'I guess so.' Robert was sullen. He scowled. 'And it would be a damn sight easier if she didn't drag Lynch to every bloody meeting we have.'

Fliss took a steadying breath. 'You don't like him much, do you?'

'No.'

She moistened her lips, aware that she was treading on dangerous ground, but compelled to ask the question just the same. 'Um—why?'

'You ask me that?' Robert was indignant, and for a moment Fliss was afraid she had said too much. But his next words relieved her of that particular fear while imbuing her with an impending sense of dread. 'The man's a leech, and you know it. Not content with making a fool of my mother, he's made a nuisance of himself with you and your father. Not to mention looking at you as if he can't wait to get your clothes off. He's a crook, Fliss. I knew it as soon as I saw him. God knows what hold he's got over Rose Chen, but if I have anything to do with it he won't get a penny out of us!'

'And what exactly do you do, um—Fliss?' inquired Rose Chen lightly, and Fliss immediately felt totally useless.

'I—help my father,' she replied at last, aware that the Chinese woman's question had been inspired more by a desire to embarrass her than by any real interest in her activities. Tonight, there was an edge of hardness about Rose Chen that boded ill for anyone who crossed her, and the fact that her purple cheongsam clashed outrageously with Fliss's dress could not have slipped her notice.

'You help your father?' she echoed scornfully. 'You mean, you don't have a career of your own?'

'No.' Fliss refused to be provoked by the other woman's rudeness. 'My mother died when I was at college, and my father took it rather badly.'

Rose Chen grimaced. 'You English,' she said, as if those two words explained everything, and despite her determination to remain immune to anything that was said Fliss had to respond.

'I know,' she said ruefully, as if Rose Chen hadn't just insulted her. 'It must be hard for you to understand. I can hardly believe you're half-English yourself.'

The barb found its mark, and Rose Chen's lips thinned. 'Oh, but I am,' she said. 'Believe it. Your boyfriend does. Hasn't he told you I'm more like our father than any of his English offspring?'

'I believe he has said that you're a fairly tough customer,' agreed Fliss, drawn into the fray in spite of herself. 'Tell me, is that a Chinese characteristic? Toughness? A lack of femininity?'

'Why, you——'

Heaven knew what Rose Chen might have said then, and Fliss, who already knew she had gone too far, was girding herself for a full-frontal attack, when another voice intervened.

'Making friends?'

Oliver Lynch's mocking tones might have been the last ones Fliss wanted to hear, but in the present circumstances she would have welcomed any interruption, and Rose Chen's features underwent a remarkable, and instantaneous, change.

'Sort of,' she said, the edge in her voice giving way to a silky purr. 'Where've you been, baby? I missed you.'

Fliss looked away in some distaste as Rose Chen slid her arm through Oliver's dark-clad sleeve and rubbed herself against him. Oh, God, she thought desperately, where was Robert, never mind anyone else? Since their arrival some fifteen minutes ago he had deserted her to attend to some request of his mother's, and she had been left in the doubtful company of his half-sister.

'I was finding some place to park the car,' she heard Oliver say carelessly, his lazily attractive baritone reminding her of how a certain hoarseness had entered his voice when he was making love. She shuddered. Dear God, how could he stand there and let Rose Chen crawl all over him when he must know how it made her feel? Did he get some perverse thrill out of seeing her squirm? 'Is there anything to drink around here?'

'Of course.'

Rose Chen detached herself long enough to bring him a scotch over ice, and Fliss pretended to be looking for something in her clutch bag until the other woman came back.

But she couldn't ignore him, not without attracting some curiosity. And she couldn't walk away from them without the other woman thinking she had frightened her. So, as there was still no sign of Robert, and his mother's other guests hadn't yet arrived, she felt obliged to offer some remark, however trivial.

But, she unfortunately chose a moment when Rose Chen was using the excuse of straightening his tie to stroke blood-red nails along his jawline, and Fliss's unwary gaze met only Oliver's pale wolf's eyes. Met— and was held by the compelling awareness of a sensuality only lightly veiled. His eyes drifted deliberately downwards. Over the dusky V of her cleavage, pausing for a moment to enjoy the sudden palpitation his appraisal had evoked. Then, reluctantly onwards, over the hands she had clasped tightly, and revealingly, at her waist, before seeking the unknowingly voluptuous curve of her hips.

Fliss's breath came in short, shallow gulps, the words she might have spoken stifled by her emotions. How could he look at her like that? How *dared* he look at her like that, with Rose Chen's face only inches from his? He had only to turn his head for Rose Chen to fasten her mouth to his, a fact he must be as aware of as Fliss was.

'All alone?' he queried, in a voice that would have melted ice-caps, and although it clearly wasn't to her liking the Chinese woman was forced to turn around, too.

'I—no,' Fliss was beginning, when Rose Chen intervened.

'Robert's opening the wine for his mother, so Fliss and I were keeping each other company, weren't we?' she asked silkily, daring the other woman to contradict her. 'I was just asking her what people do for entertainment in this rustic backwater. But apparently Fliss likes it. She doesn't even go out to work.'

Fliss's cheeks coloured. 'I was just explaining that I work for my father,' she declared, hating the way she felt obliged to defend her position, but to her dismay Oliver chose to support her.

'Yes,' he said, addressing his remarks to Rose Chen, 'the Reverend's something of an historian. Fliss is helping him write a book about the history of the village. He was telling me about it, when we had tea together. Isn't that right—Fliss?'

'Well—OK.' To her relief, Rose Chen chose to put an end to that particular topic, though the look she cast in Fliss's direction was in no way conciliatory. 'Who cares, anyway? As far as I'm concerned, I prefer a little more action in my life.' Her lips took on a sensuous slant. 'And in my men,' she appended, fingerwalking up Oliver's chest. 'Well, one man, at least.'

Fliss turned away again, and to her relief she saw her fiancé coming towards them. He didn't look pleased to see her with Rose Chen and Oliver Lynch, but in Fliss's opinion even looking at his dour countenance was preferable to being an unwilling voyeur to the other couple's flirtation.

'Well, here you are again, Lynch,' Robert greeted the older man coldly. 'I'd have thought you'd be heading back to Hong Kong by now. Isn't that where the action is? According to my sister, you find us a pretty boring substitute.'

Fliss felt her own nerves tighten then, half in resentment, half in apprehension, but Oliver only shrugged his broad shoulders. Unlike Robert, who was wearing a dinner-jacket, he was dressed in a charcoal lounge suit this evening, the sombre colour only adding to his dark attraction.

'Did Rose say that?' he responded, without rancour, as the woman in question gave Robert a killing look. 'No, I'm not bored. How could I be, in such delightful company?'

Robert's brows lowered. 'What's that supposed to mean?' he demanded suspiciously, and Oliver gave him an innocent smile.

'It doesn't—mean—anything more than it says,' he essayed easily. 'Your fiancée was kind enough to introduce me to her father the other day, and one way and another I'm beginning to feel really at home.'

'Yes—well, I wanted to talk to you about that,' said Robert aggressively, and, realising she couldn't allow this to deteriorate into a slanging match, Fliss intervened.

'Did I tell you Mr Lynch shares Daddy's interest in history?' she exclaimed, addressing her remarks to Rose Chen, even though she was sure the Chinese woman had no interest in her conversation. She moistened her lips. 'When he was studying law at Harvard, he——'

'Hold it!' Before she could go any further, Rose Chen turned to the man beside her. 'You studied *law* at Harvard?' she exclaimed disbelievingly. 'You didn't tell me that, Lee.'

'Didn't I?' Fliss had the sudden impression that Oliver was disconcerted now. But he quickly recovered himself, spreading his hands in a careless gesture. 'Hey, I told you I dropped out. Where the hell d'you think I dropped out from? High school?'

'I don't know.' Clearly Rose Chen was having some difficulty dealing with this revelation. 'I guess I thought——' She broke off and shook her head. 'But— Harvard! It costs a lot of money to go there, doesn't it?'

'Why do you think I dropped out?' exclaimed Oliver, rolling his eyes, but Fliss wasn't deceived by his bland dismissal of his past. She was fairly sure he hadn't wanted Rose Chen to know that particular piece of his history, though why that should be so she couldn't imagine.

# CHAPTER SEVEN

BUT, before Robert could take him up on it too, the doorbell rang, heralding the arrival of Mrs Hastings' other guests. The local doctor and his wife, plus the owner of a nearby stud farm and his live-in girlfriend, put an end to any intimate conversation, and Fliss found herself accepting another glass of white wine and assuring Dr Carpenter that her father was in the best of health.

All the same, she found her eyes following Oliver as he accompanied Rose Chen around the room. Whatever her personal feelings, Robert's mother was making a concerted effort to behave as if she had accepted the situation, and her acknowledgement of Rose Chen was obviously going a long way to legitimising her position. In consequence, her introductions were, if not warm, then at least cordial. And, although Rose Chen had expressed contempt for village life, she evidently saw the sense in not antagonising anybody.

The final guest to arrive was Ralph Williams, the owner of a large estate that bordered on Sutton Magna, and a local magistrate. A widower for several years, he considered himself the most eligible bachelor hereabouts, and although Fliss knew he had only been invited to even the numbers he was blind to any indignity.

'Smug devil,' Robert exhorted, glowering as the new arrival hung on to Rose Chen's hand rather longer than was necessary. 'Can't he see what a fool he's making of himself? She's not going to look at him with Lynch breathing down her neck.'

Fliss endeavoured to speak casually. 'Is—Mr Lynch breathing down her neck?' She hesitated. 'He appears to be talking to your mother.'

'Mmm.' Robert grunted. 'He's a regular charmer, isn't he? They both are. Like snakes!'

'Oh, Rob——'

'Well.' He swallowed the remainder of the scotch in his glass, and Fliss wondered how many he had had. 'Just because I have to go along with this, it doesn't mean I like it. And if that—that—creep—speaks to you one more time——'

'Rob, please.' She sighed. 'Why can't we just forget Oliver Lynch for the rest of the evening? He's not important. Can't you see that?'

Robert scowled. 'I don't like him. I don't like his attitude. And I particularly don't like your father telling me what an interesting fellow he is.'

Fliss swallowed. 'Did Daddy say that?'

'Yes.' Robert hunched his shoulders in an aggressive gesture. 'He spoke as if Lynch was making some useful contribution to the world, while I was just one of life's hangers-on!'

'Oh, Rob, I'm sure he didn't say that.'

'No, he didn't say it. It's just implicit in what he does say. I wonder sometimes if he even likes me. He's never referred to me as an "interesting fellow". Not in my hearing, anyway.'

Fliss was relieved when the Hastingses' housekeeper came to announce that dinner was served, and she could abandon any attempt to restore Robert's good humour and concentrate on the food. The meal would be over soon, she consoled herself. And if Amanda Hastings had anything to do with it there was no chance that Oliver Lynch would be sitting anywhere near her.

He wasn't. With Mrs Hastings occupying one end of the table, and Robert taking his father's place at the other, they were at least two places diagonally across from one another. Although Amanda had been forced to place Rose Chen at her right hand, she had positioned Oliver on her left, with the undemanding presence of Mrs Carpenter on his other side. Fliss, meanwhile, was next to Robert, with Dr Carpenter opposite and Brian Vasey, the stud owner, and his girlfriend, Lucy Wales, occupying the middle ground. Ralph Williams, who might have expected to sit next to his hostess, was on Rose Chen's other side, and no doubt Robert's mother hoped he would take care of her so that she had Oliver all to herself.

Thinking this, Fliss realised how ridiculous it was that she should even be making such a deduction. It was nothing to do with her how Amanda Hastings conducted herself, even if monopolising her escort was no way to win Rose Chen's confidence.

A creamy asparagus mousse, wrapped in smoked salmon, preceded a crisp rack of lamb, and Fliss made a concerted effort to enjoy it. Mrs Hughes, the Hastings' housekeeper, always prepared such delicious meals, and this evening she had the help of her niece to serve the food.

Alison Hughes was a pretty girl in her teens, who was evidently just as susceptible to Oliver's charm as her employer. She coloured becomingly when he made some comment as she removed his plate, and her smile only disappeared when she caught Amanda Hastings' eye. The fact that Fliss was aware of this, and of Rose Chen's less than friendly reaction to the exchange, only added to her own feelings of frustration. She couldn't wait for the meal to be over so that she could escape her treacherous observations.

'I haven't seen you at the stables recently, Fliss,' Brian Vasey remarked, as he carved the pink flesh on his plate. As well as breeding horses he also ran a fairly successful riding stables, and from time to time Fliss hired a mount and went hacking.

'No.' Fliss was glad of the diversion. 'It's been so hot, and what with one thing and another...'

'You mean this business over James's will, don't you?' Brain murmured, his tone low enough not to attract attention. 'Must have been quite a shock when—she—turned up.'

'Mmm.'

Fliss didn't want to get into a discussion about that, but she couldn't prevent the involuntary glance she cast towards the other end of the table. And, although Oliver had his head bent towards his hostess, evidently listening to something she was saying, and couldn't possibly have overheard Brian's remark, he looked up at that moment and intercepted her gaze.

She looked away at once, one hand going nervously to the gold ring suspended from her ear, but not before Oliver's eyes had narrowed perceptively. And, even though she consoled herself with the thought that she had done nothing wrong, she hoped no one else had noticed the exchange.

'I like your dress,' Lucy Wales complimented her from across the table. An attractive blonde in her late thirties, Lucy had been with Brian for more than fifteen years, and although their relationship had raised a few eyebrows when they first came to live in the village, these days it was accepted that they were as much of a pair as any married couple. They had no children, and as far as Fliss knew they had no intention of having any. Which, in her view, constituted the main reason why people should seek the endorsement of the church. 'That colour really suits you,' Lucy added, guilelessly. 'You've got such gorgeous skin!'

Fliss felt the hot colour invade her cheeks. She was aware that Lucy's voice had carried clearly round the room. Everyone, including Oliver Lynch, she saw unhappily, was looking in her direction now, and she offered a muttered disclaimer before resuming her efforts to eat the food on her plate. But she knew that at least two of the women present resented her unsought notoriety. Rose Chen looked as if she didn't appreciate any bid to divert attention from herself as the guest of honour, and Mrs Hastings obviously considered it an unnecessary intrusion. But then, Lucy was not one of her favourite people, and she only tolerated her because Brian was such a useful addition to her dinner parties.

'I've got good taste, haven't I?' Robert remarked smugly, prolonging Fliss's embarrassment. 'Unlike——'

Whether he had been about to say his father, Fliss didn't wait to find out. She knew Robert had been drinking fairly steadily since they arrived, and his wine glass had been refilled several times as well. Judging by the hectic colour in his cheeks, he was well on his way to reaching his limit, and when Robert was drunk, he didn't care what he said.

'Unlike me, do you mean?' she interrupted him lightly, deliberately softening her remark with an intimate squeezing of his hand. 'Why don't you pay me compliments like that, darling? Don't I deserve them?'

Robert stared at her with blank eyes for a moment. Her behaviour was so unlike the Fliss he was used to, that his muddled brain couldn't immediately cope with the change. But when she tried to withdraw her hand again, he seemed to come to his senses. Turning his hand over, he grasped her fingers, holding on to them forcefully, causing her to wince.

'Is that what you want?' he demanded in a low voice, and Fliss, who only wanted to escape now, gave him a nervous smile.

'All I want at the moment is my hand back, please,' she exclaimed, forcing herself to sustain her girlish character. 'Rob, you're hurting me. Let me go. I want to finish my dinner.'

Robert looked as if he might resist, and she was wishing Lucy had never said anything when he let her go. And, as she thrust her numb fingers below the level of the tablecloth, she was aware that Oliver Lynch had observed the whole incident. His pale eyes mirrored an expression of anger or contempt or both, and she guessed he despised her for making such an exhibition of herself.

The fact that it hadn't been her fault, and that she had only been trying to prevent any further unpleasantness, wouldn't occur to him. As far as he was concerned, she had proved her weakness by the fact that Robert obviously knew nothing about what had occurred in the kitchen at the vicarage.

The meal dragged to its inevitable close, and when Mrs Hastings suggested they all adjourn to the drawing-room for coffee Fliss couldn't wait to find a quiet corner, where she could regain a little of her anonymity. She wasn't used to being the centre of attraction, and she hoped Robert wouldn't do anything else to embarrass her.

To her relief, his mother must have realised her son had been in danger of embarrassing her, too, not to mention antagonising the one person they could least afford to antagonise, if they hoped to retain any measure of credibility here. While Fliss accompanied the other guests into the lamplit drawing-room, Amanda Hastings carried her son off to the kitchen, ostensibly to get the coffee. But, privately, Fliss suspected his mother's intentions had more to do with sobering him up than a desire for his assistance.

In consequence, Fliss was free to seek the window seat, installing herself on its padded bench in such a way as to discourage anyone else from joining her. Outside it was just beginning to get dark, enabling her to see her reflection in the shadowed pane. Was that wild-eyed stranger really her? she wondered unhappily. Where was the languid-lidded woman she used to be? When had she changed from cool indifference to feverish panic?

She saw his reflection in the darkened window before she was obliged to turn her head and feign surprise. His tall, broad-shouldered frame was unmistakable—at least, to someone who had thought about little else but him all evening.

'Slipped the leash?' Oliver enquired, with scarcely veiled insolence. 'After that little display at the dinner table, I'm surprised he isn't dragging you up the stairs to his bedroom?'

Fliss cast a horrified glance about her, but to her relief there was no one else within earshot. 'What do you want?' she asked, in a low incensed tone. 'Do you make an effort to be rude, or does it just come naturally to you?'

'I'm working on it,' replied Oliver shortly. 'So where is he? Sleeping off the effects of the two bottles of Chablis he consumed at dinner?'

'He's helping his mother get the coffee, as a matter of fact,' retorted Fliss, biting her tongue when Mrs Hughes and her niece appeared with two trays. As there was still no sign of her fiancé, that was patently not his mission, and Oliver's lips twisted as he recognised her plight.

'OK,' he said, turning with the obvious intention of seating himself beside her, and Fliss was obliged to shuffle along the bench to make room for him, 'so do you want to tell me how you came to be involved with that p—idiot?'

Fliss closed her eyes for a moment, realising there was no point in trying to reason with him. In fact, there was no talking to him at all, and instead of answering she looked pointedly across the room.

'The silent treatment, hmm?' he said softly, putting his hand down and covering the hand she had used to edge herself out of his way. She was still gripping the edge of the cushion, half prepared to find somewhere else to sit. But as she'd had no wish to draw any more attention to herself, she'd hesitated. She'd been unaware of her vulnerability until he'd touched her.

'Don't!' she exclaimed instantly, snatching her hand away and imprisoning both hands between her knees. 'Why don't you go and torment your girlfriend?'

'You didn't like it when I did,' he declared softly, and although he wasn't touching her now, Fliss felt as if he was. Her palms grew so sticky, they felt as if they were glued together, and their reaction spread along her legs and centred in the moist heat between her thighs.

'I couldn't care less what you do,' she told him, not altogether truthfully, aware that Rose Chen had noticed Oliver's whereabouts and was watching them with a gimlet gaze. But unfortunately Brian Vasey had engaged her in conversation, and she was apparently unwilling to be rude to the handsome horse trainer. Fliss took a steadying breath. 'Aren't you afraid she'll—object to your neglecting her?'

'Oh, I don't neglect Rose,' he assured her, with infuriating candour. 'I admit, she can be a little—possessive. But nothing I can't handle.'

Fliss sucked in her stomach. 'You're disgusting!' she exclaimed, forcing herself not to look at him and betray her real feelings to anyone else in the room. 'I can't think what she sees in you.'

'Can't you?' His voice was gently mocking now. 'Come on, Fliss. Who do you think you're fooling? Me? Or yourself?'

Fliss gasped. 'How dare you?'

'How dare I what? Remind you that you're not as composed—*controlled*—as you'd like to think? You may look as if you've got a mouthful of ice-cubes, but we both know better than that. That's why I find you so irresistible. You're such a delicious mix of virgin and wanton!'

Fliss couldn't listen to any more of this. With a feeling akin to panic she made to get up, only to find her progress impeded by his fingers clutching a handful of her skirt.

'Where are you going?' he protested, when she was compelled to turn desperate eyes in his direction. 'Don't look at me like that. Do you want Rose to think there's something going on between us? She's already suspicious. I'd hate her to feel she had a need to get her claws into you. Literally, I mean.'

Fliss stared at him. 'You don't give up, do you?' She forced herself to stay calm. 'And don't transfer your own fears on to me. It's your eyes she'd scratch out, not mine.'

'Think so?' Oliver was unrepentant. 'What an innocent world you live in, Fliss. My punishment would be much less respectable. There are other parts of my anatomy Rose would aim for. Believe me, she takes no prisoners.'

'Takes no prisoners?' Fliss looked blank for a moment, and then the realisation that he was mocking her brought the hot colour into her neck again. 'Oh—go away' she hissed, intensely aware that the hand tangled in her skirt was also uncomfortably close to her thigh. 'I really don't want to discuss it.'

'Nor do I,' he declared mildly, confounding her resistance. 'Now, here comes Alison with our coffee. You're not going to walk out on me, are you?'

Fliss was torn between the need to put some space between them so that she could get things into perspective again, and the awareness that any move on her part now would look strange. As far as the other guests were concerned, they appeared to be having a perfectly innocent conversation, and it seemed the lesser of two evils to stay where she was.

'Just sugar, thanks,' Oliver said, when the young waitress served his coffee. 'That's great. You're doing a good job.'

'Thanks, Mr Lynch.'

Alison was clearly fascinated by the dark stranger, and Fliss had to bite her tongue again to prevent herself from commenting on it after she had gone. She had no wish for Oliver to think she cared one way or the other. All the same, deep down, a tiny spark of irritation flamed, and she had to tamp it down firmly before it ignited.

'Why didn't you tell Robert I—touched you?' he asked suddenly, his soft voice startling her. And Fliss, who had been congratulating herself on her restraint, returned her coffee-cup to its saucer with rather more force than she'd intended.

'Can we just forget all about that, please?' she said, through her teeth. 'I think we've agreed that it should never have happened, and I see no reason in upsetting Rob over something so trivial.'

'Was it?' he persisted huskily. 'Trivial, I mean? I don't believe that.'

'I don't care what you believe.' Fliss could hear her voice rising in concert with the shallowness of her breathing. She struggled to control herself, and then went on unevenly, 'I don't want you to mention this ever— ever again, do you hear me? You have your life, and I have mine. I'd be grateful if you'd respect that.'

'So prim,' mocked Oliver, setting his cup aside. 'No wonder Robert guards you like the crown jewels. He must think you've never——'

'Now, isn't this cosy?'

Rose Chen came sauntering towards them on spiky heels. With a complete disregard for Fliss's feelings, she manoeuvred herself between them, perching on Oliver's knee, and draping her arm around his neck. Then, with her possession clearly staked, she permitted Fliss a triumphant smile.

'Don't believe a word he says,' she added, scraping her nail over Oliver's roughening jawline. 'He's a real bastard. And I can vouch for it.'

Well, you'd know, Fliss wanted to say cattily, and was appalled at the instinct she had to play the other woman at her own game. Apart from anything else, she wasn't like that. She had never been like that. Jealousy simply wasn't part of her make-up, and it was infuriating to think that she was even entertaining such emotions about Oliver Lynch.

'Um—Mr Lynch and I were just talking about—indoor sports,' she offered, and then wished she'd chosen to say anything but that when both Rose Chen and Oliver gave her an amused look.

'Oh, we know all about them, don't we, Lee?' the Chinese woman declared mockingly. 'What particular indoor sport did you have in mind? Is it a ball game.'

'It was cards, actually,' lied Fliss, refusing to let them make a fool of her yet again. 'Excuse me. I must go and find Robert.'

'Try the john,' called Rose Chen, as she walked away, and Fliss's skin crawled at the burst of laughter that followed her. It was all she could do not to head for the door and freedom, and she was inestimably relieved when Robert himself appeared, looking pale but composed.

'Are you all right?' Fliss asked, going up to him, and Robert gave her an aggrieved look.

'Why shouldn't I be?' he demanded. 'Just because I needed a bit of fresh air, don't you get on my back as well.'

'As well?' Fliss frowned.

'As my mother,' retorted Robert, glancing half apprehensively over his shoulder. 'The old girl seemed to think I was in danger of insulting the old man. Though why she should worry, I don't know.'

Fliss doubted Amanda Hastings would appreciate her son's description of her, but she was too eager to leave to waste time taking him up on it.

'Can we go now?' she asked. 'I—actually, I've got a bit of a headache myself.'

'Leave?' echoed Robert, looking round the room. 'I've only just got here. Where's the coffee? I could surely use a cup.'

Fliss sighed. 'Over there,' she said wearily, gesturing to where Mrs Hughes and her niece had left the trays. 'Rob——'

But Robert was already threading his way across the room, exchanging a word here and there as he headed for his objective. For the moment she was on her own, and with a determined stiffening of her spine she walked out of the room.

She met Mrs Hastings in the hall outside. Robert's mother was checking her hair in the mirror above a small occasional table, and she looked rather irritably at Fliss when she appeared.

'Couldn't you have stopped Rob from making such a fool of himself?' she demanded, launching immediately into an attack, and Fliss stepped back in surprise.

'Making a fool——'

'Drinking too much,' snapped Amanda Hastings impatiently. 'You know what Rob's like when he drinks too much.'

'No. I——'

'He's indiscreet,' the older woman stated grimly. 'I almost died when *he* said he had good taste. You must have noticed.'

'Well, yes——'

'Very well, then. We'll have to make sure it doesn't happen again. Not when Rose Chen is here anyway.' She took a breath, as if mentally shifting into another gear. 'Now—where are you going?'

Fliss swallowed. 'The—the bathroom?'

'Mmm.' Mrs Hastings nodded. 'All right.'

'Then I thought we might—go,' Fliss ventured carefully.

'We?'

'Robert and me.'

Mrs Hastings snorted. 'You don't expect him to drive you home? Not in his condition!'

'No.' In truth, Fliss had been so intent on getting away, she hadn't considered the mechanics of it. 'Well—I can wait——'

'Nonsense. Brian Vasey can take you. It's hardly out of their way.'

'Oh—really——'

'No. That's settled.' Mrs Hastings sniffed and regarded Fliss with some irritation. 'Well? What are you waiting for? I thought you wanted to go to the bathroom.'

'Oh, yes.' Fliss nodded, and went obediently up the stairs.

But, in the bathroom, common sense reasserted itself, and she gazed at her reflection in the mirror with some amazement. Honestly, she had let Robert's mother speak to her as if she was about five years old. Was that really how Mrs Hastings saw her? As an ineffectual female, incapable of speaking up for herself, or fighting back?

She sighed. The fact that the conversation she had had with Oliver Lynch had left her in a state of some confusion had to bear some of the burden, of course. But she was getting sick of being made to feel as if she didn't have the guts to organise her own life, and after pushing a few errant hairs back into place she went determinedly downstairs again.

This time, Robert met her at the door of the drawing-room, his hand fastening possessively about her arm as she came in. 'Where have you been?' he demanded aggressively, as if he hadn't disappeared for the best part of half an hour earlier in the evening.

'I found I needed some air, too,' replied Fliss, with unaccustomed arrogance. 'And now I'm leaving, with or without your permission.'

Robert frowned. 'Is something wrong?'

'No.' Fliss had no intention of voicing her grievances here. 'I just want to go home, that's all. Now, if you'll let me go, I'll say my goodnights.'

Robert gazed at her. 'OK.' He moistened his lips as he released her arm. 'I'll just tell my mother we're leaving and then I'll get the car.'

'No.' Fliss looked up at him coldly. 'You've been drinking, Robert. You can walk me home, if you like, but you obviously can't drive.'

'Now, wait——'

'What's going on here?'

As if sensitive to her son's mood, Mrs Hastings appeared beside them, and Robert turned to her with ill-concealed fury. 'Did you tell Fliss I couldn't take her home?'

Flashing her future daughter-in-law a malevolent glance, Amanda Hastings clicked her tongue. 'I may have done,' she said quietly. Then, to Fliss, 'I was just about to ask Brian——'

'Vasey?'

'Is something wrong?'

Rose Chen joined them then, her curiosity evidently getting the better of her, and Mrs Hastings regarded her with tight lips. 'No,' she said, forcing herself to speak cordially. She glanced at Oliver Lynch who had appeared behind the Chinese woman. 'Oh—are you leaving?'

'We thought we might,' Rose Chen agreed, slipping her arm through Oliver's, as if she felt the need to hold on to him. 'It's been a delightful evening, Mandy. I do appreciate it.'

'Think nothing of it,' said Mrs Hastings, looking as if she had just swallowed a lemon. 'We must do it again.'

'No. Next time you must let us entertain you,' declared Rose Chen, including Oliver in the invitation deliberately, Fliss was sure. She looked at the English girl then. 'Lovely to see you again—um—Fluff.'

There was a moment's silence, when they all acknowledged the slight that had just been delivered, and then Oliver said levelly, 'Perhaps we can give you a lift home, Fliss. I believe I heard you say something about walking, but I was sitting by the window, and I believe it's started to rain.'

'Oh, I——'

'I'm sure—Fliss—would rather her fiancé escorted her home,' inserted Rose Chen quickly, but for once Mrs Hastings chose not to take her son's part.

'That sounds like a very good idea,' she said, ignoring the outraged face her son turned in her direction. 'Don't you agree, Fliss?'

And, although Fliss had sworn never to be put in such a situation again, there was absolutely nothing she could do.

# CHAPTER EIGHT

THE Mercedes moved smoothly beneath his hands, the thick leather cool beneath his jean-clad thighs. Although he knew it was crazy, and he was quite aware that he was breaking the speed limit, he let the powerful vehicle make its own pace, the road passing beneath the big car's wheels at an ever-increasing rate.

It felt so good to be out on his own, away from Rose Chen's cloying presence, and if it wasn't really her fault that he felt this way it was easier to blame her than acknowledge what was really wrong with him.

Yet he was acknowledging it, Oliver thought drily. By just being on the road, heading for Sutton Magna, he was tacitly accepting that the reason for his uncertain temper was a cool almost-blonde temptress, whose eyes and lips, and lush, golden body, were threatening his hard-won impassivity.

He could imagine how Lightfoot would react if he knew his errant operative was in danger of blowing the whole deal on account of his hormones. If he even suspected that Oliver was risking the relationship he had built up with Rose Chen because he could think of little else but burying his aching sex in another woman's slick moist sheath, he'd have a seizure.

But God, it was years since he'd lain awake nights, imagining how it would feel to make it with some special woman. Hell, he'd been a kid when that happened, still bemused by his own feelings, and eager to lay every chick in sight. Until Louise, and that abortive teenage marriage, that had taught him there was more to a relationship than relieving his frustration. He was too wise now to act like a lovesick moron; too old to have wet dreams.

The fact remained, he was risking everything for a woman who hated his guts. Or acted as if she did, anyway. A woman who was already involved with another man. And that man, moreover, who was one of the prime suspects in his investigation.

He thumped the wheel with the flat of his hand, his jaw hardening as he unwillingly considered the facts of the case again. If Robert Hastings wasn't involved, then he was more sinned against than sinning. But could he really be that naïve? He was James Hastings' son, for pity's sake! Who should have been more equipped to take his father's place than his only son? The twins were obviously too young, and there was no one else. Except Rose...

Oliver's mouth compressed. So far, he had no real evidence to connect Rose Chen to the operation. But, unlike her half-brother, there was nothing naïve about her, and Oliver had no doubt now that she had been involved. Was still involved, for all he knew.

For instance, he suspected she was the only one, apart from James Hastings himself, who knew what was on the computer disk he had seen her reading after the office was closed the other evening. He'd only glimpsed its contents from a distance, but it had looked like a spreadsheet. He guessed it contained at least some of the information he was looking for. If only he'd had the chance to read it.

Chance, he mused wryly. So much of life—so much of his work—relied on chance, and he was a great believer in taking whatever was offered you. It was only chance that had brought him to the office, looking for Rose Chen; only chance that he'd come upon her using ne of the firm's computers, when until then he hadn't en known she could operate one.

And it hadn't taken a great leap of intelligence to realise that this could be the break he was looking for, and the fact that Rose had quickly closed down the programme and turned off the computer had only confirmed his suspicions. Yet, to someone not looking for trouble, her attitude had been merely apologetic, the face she turned to him entreating his understanding that she had simply forgotten the time.

He believed that. He believed she had been so involved with what she was reading that she had forgotten the time. But she had made a mistake in drawing attention to herself; had proved she had something to hide in the hastiness of her actions.

Still, so long as she trusted him, she wouldn't suspect he might use the information against her. So far as she was concerned he had been more concerned with missing his dinner than wondering what she was doing. He was just one of life's drifters, after all. Why should he care if she acted a little nervously? What was it to him if she slipped the disk unobtrusively into her handbag?

Since then, he'd not seen the disk again. Even though he'd searched her apartment quite assiduously, and rifled the desk in her office. And it was a precarious business, making sure he left everything as he found it. Particularly at the office, when he had known he could be disturbed at any time.

But he'd chosen an afternoon when Rose had been entertaining Maurice Willis, of Willis antiques, ostensibly one of the firm's largest clients, who took many of the gold and bronze artefacts Hastings' imported into the country. Only Oliver knew Willis was not one of their largest clients—at least, not in the business with which James Hastings had amassed his fortune. His big clients were grey, unassuming men you'd pass in the street without noticing, not bluff, noisy giants who called Rose 'little lady' and drank more than was good for them.

Even so, his investigations had all been for nothing. He'd found nothing of a suspicious nature, and he'd come to the conclusion that if Rose still had the disk she was either concealing it about her person or keeping it in her handbag. Besides, he had no concrete proof that the disk bore any incriminating evidence whatsoever. James Hastings had survived in this business for more than fifteen years that they knew of, and he hadn't done that by being indiscreet.

Which was the reason why he was in England, Oliver acknowledged grimly. The colonel wasn't a fool either, and he knew that his best chance of nailing the operation was by getting someone so close to the source that they themselves became incriminated. *Ergo*, Oliver's increasingly reluctant relationship with Rose Chen. And although that evening when she had seemed close to confiding in him hadn't been repeated, he knew if he played his cards right it was only a matter of time before she trusted him completely. If Robert Hastings wasn't involved, who else did she have? However sick it made him feel, she was in love with him.

He sighed. Yet he was jeopardising the whole project by pursuing a woman who'd rather he didn't exist. He had no illusions about what Fliss thought of him. She might respond to his kisses, might lose that cool composure in the undoubted heat of their lovemaking, but she'd fight him every inch of the way. She was content with her life here. She didn't want an affair that exploded all the careful myths she'd cultivated about herself. But, whether she liked it or not, her world was already changing, and, once the authorities were given the proof they needed, Robert, Amanda, and the other Hastingses couldn't help being caught in the crossfire.

So what was he doing here? he asked himself harshly. Whatever happened, Fliss was unlikely to want to see im, before or after the holocaust. Dammit, she was just likely to blame him for what happened. Whatever he thought of her relationship with Robert Hastings, she thought she loved him, and she wouldn't forgive anyone for destroying what was left of his inheritance.

Oliver scowled. He knew all this; he knew a washed-up Vietnam vet had absolutely nothing in common with an English vicar's daughter, yet he couldn't leave her alone. He was risking his relationship with Rose, his job, maybe even his life, if the men who controlled the British end of the operation thought he knew too much for his own good; and there was nothing he could do about it.

It was a little before eleven as he drove along the high street in Sutton Magna. The traffic in the village wasn't heavy, but there were one or two cars parked outside the general stores, and a handful of dogs vied for ownership of the green while their owners stood gossiping. No one appeared to take any particular notice of the Mercedes. He just hoped Amanda Hastings didn't do her shopping in Sutton Magna.

The church was at the end of the village, standing in its own grounds, which in turn adjoined the garden of the vicarage. An elderly man was busy trimming the hedge that fronted the old Victorian building, and as it was a fairly warm day he didn't mind at all when Oliver parked the car and came round to speak to him.

'Miss Hayton?' the man said, wiping his sweating forehead with the kind of coloured kerchief Oliver had always thought was reserved for neck-ties. 'Oh, you mean Fliss. Yes, she's about somewhere. Just brought me a cup of coffee, she did.' He nodded towards the empty mug residing on his wheelbarrow. 'Just what I needed, you know. Cold drinks don't cool you down, did you know that? It's proven fact——'

'I'll just go and see if I can find her,' Oliver broke in politely, thinking that a long cold beer would suit *him* very well. 'Thanks,' he added, opening the gate. Then, because he felt guilty at having cut the garrulous old gardener short, he indicated the hedge. 'Good job!'

'A *hot* job,' amended the old man, taking off his cap for a moment, and wiping the kerchief over his balding pate. He frowned. 'You that American who was here having tea with the vicar a week or so ago?'

Oliver gave an inward groan. He'd forgotten how small towns—*villages*, in this country—wanted to know everything about you. In Maple Falls, Virginia, you couldn't paint your fence without someone giving you advice about the colour.

'Yeah. Right,' he agreed, starting up the paved path, and although he was sure the gardener would have liked to continue the conversation he deliberately refrained from looking back.

Fliss herself answered his ring, and he could tell at once that she had known it was him before she opened the door. And why not? he asked himself wryly. He hadn't exactly disguised his arrival. She must have seen him from the window, and she was breathing rather fast, as if she had run down the stairs to prevent either her father or the housekeeper from intercepting him.

'Hi,' he said, thinking how pleasant it was to find a woman who didn't spend all her days in trousers. Her full-skirted print dress was rather longer than he could have wished, hiding as it did those gorgeous legs. But its strappy top exposed her arms and shoulders, and they were a delicious shade of honey. She had tied her hair back today. A french braid exposed the delicate curve of her profile, and the fine strands that had escaped at her hairline were dewy with moisture. 'Surprised to see me?'

'Not exactly.'

It wasn't quite the greeting he had hoped for, but he was nothing if not a realist. 'Is that good or bad? Were you expecting me?'

Fliss's tongue circled her upper lip, and Oliver quelled the urge he had to capture its pink tip between his teeth.

'I was afraid you might come back,' she said coolly. 'What do you want?'

Oliver put one foot on the step that led up to the porch, and tucked his thumbs securely in the back of his belt. 'Do I have to answer that?' he asked ruefully, aware of her wary withdrawal. 'How are you? How's your father?'

'I hope you don't really expect me to believe you care,' she exclaimed. 'But——' as good manners got the better of her '—he's very well, actually. As I was until I saw you.'

Oliver's lips twitched. 'You don't pull your punches, do you?' He grimaced. 'I guess you're still mad at me for the other evening. I thought you'd be glad of a lift. As you didn't even have a coat.'

Fliss took a deep breath. 'Your concern was overwhelming. It didn't occur to you that I might not want to get into a car with that—coarse female you call a girlfriend?'

'Rose?' He shrugged. 'I admit, she can be a bit bitchy at times.' He paused. 'She's just jealous.'

Fliss gasped. 'You arrogant——'

'Of you,' he informed her flatly. 'Rose has never met anyone like you before.' His lips twisted. 'I guess I could say the same.'

'I bet you could.' Fliss's face had filled with becoming colour. 'And if you think flattery——'

'Damn!' The word was out before Oliver could prevent it, and with a gesture of self-loathing he dragged his gaze away from her face. Then, trying to compose himself, 'I didn't come here to have an argument.'

'What did you come here for?'

'To see you,' he snarled, and her hand shook as it sought the frame of the door, grasping it defensively, as if she was afraid he might physically attack her.

There was silence for a few moments, and Oliver cursed himself anew for having come here. He had really blown it this time. She'd never believe he meant her no harm after this.

'You'd better come in.'

Fliss's taut voice broke into his self-flagellation. As if she had just noticed that the old gardener, who, if he couldn't actually hear what they were saying, was taking an inordinate interest in their exchange, she raised a hand to the man, and then stepped backwards away from the door.

'My—my father's not here. He's at the church,' she added, in the same strained voice. 'He—he conducts a communion service for his older parishioners on Wednesday mornings. He won't be back until twelve.'

Oliver hesitated only briefly, before crossing the tiled porch and entering the vicarage. Fliss stepped behind him to close the door, and then leaned back against it, her palms flat against the wood. Oliver turned from an involuntary appraisal of an antique chest and umbrella stand, to find her golden hair haloed by the bottle-glass panels behind her.

His heart thumped. She was so beautiful to him, so pure. He wanted to hold her, and possess her and keep her safe. Not just from Robert and Rose, and the mess James Hastings had left behind him. But from him, from himself. He was so afraid he was going to hurt her.

He knew she was aware of him, knew that inviting him inside had been an act of supreme bravery, risking as it did her behaviour's becoming a talking point in the village. The old man—the gardener—had already proved he enjoyed a good gossip. His visit here was, in its way, as dangerous to her reputation as it was to his.

But right now all that mattered was that he was here and so was she, and God help him, he couldn't keep his hands off her. Refusing to respond to the censure of his conscience, he moved towards her, supporting his weight on hands that imprisoned her within the obstruction they created, bending his head to brush her lips with his tongue.

Her breath escaped against his mouth, soft and warm and sweetly scented. She was breathing rather quickly, and although he resisted the urge to slide his hand beneath her breast and feel the rapid beating of her heart for himself, he could see the pulse palpitating at her jawline. Dammit, his own pulse was beating just as rapidly, and the womanly scent of her body only accentuated his attraction to her.

'You knew I'd come, didn't you?' he murmured, tipping one slender strap off her shoulder, and lowering his head to kiss the silken skin. His tongue moved against the soft flesh and she quivered. 'I haven't been able to think about anything else but you for the past ten days. Hell, before that. Ever since we met, actually.'

Fliss drew in an unsteady breath. 'I can't believe that,' she said tremulously, but although he moved in closer, she made no attempt to get away.

'It's true,' he told her. 'Just because I acted like an idiot that night at the Hastingses', don't think I wasn't remembering how it was between us.'

'But Rose——'

'To hell with Rose,' he muttered recklessly, bringing up his hand to run his knuckles over the downy curve of her cheek. 'I was jealous. Didn't you realise that? Whenever that—that ass-hole touched you, I wanted to put my gun between his ribs.'

'No——'

'Yes.' He was adamant. He cupped her face in his hand, rubbing his thumb insistently over the sensitive skin beneath her ear. 'And you know it. That's why we're here—why you're not fighting me any more.'

Fliss swallowed. 'I'm confused——'

'That makes two of us.' Oliver's lips took on a ruefully sensuous curve, and his thumb found her mouth. 'Oh, baby, I want you——'

'No——'

'Yes.' His eyes followed his thumb, as it smeared wetness over her lips. 'I know you're engaged to that stuffed shirt, but, isn't this more important?'

He'd gone too far. He knew it as soon as the words were uttered, and a look of distaste crossed Fliss's face. Unwittingly—unwillingly—he had reminded her of her obligations to Robert, and she stiffened automatically, pressing back against the door.

'No,' she got out unevenly. 'No, this is not more important. I don't know what you want from me, but I was a fool to let you in here and an even bigger fool to think I could trust you.'

Oliver briefly closed his eyes. 'You can trust me.'

Fliss snorted. 'To do what? To make me betray Robert? To jeopardise my marriage, just because you—you've got some kind of vendetta against him?'

Oliver groaned. 'I've got no vendetta against Hastings,' he protested. But hadn't he? Wasn't that exactly what he did have?

'Well, whatever.' Fliss moved her stiff body away from the door, and Oliver found himself straightening, pushing his hands into his pockets, letting her get past him. 'I want you to go.'

She had a dignity he couldn't fault, an hauteur he couldn't deny. And he knew if he let her walk away from him now, he might never get another chance to talk to her alone.

'Wait,' he said, taking one hand out of his pocket, and making a helpless gesture. 'Don't—don't do this.'

'Do what?' She turned to face him again, and he guessed she thought the danger was over. 'You've said what you came to say, Mr Lynch. You've succeeded in humiliating me—yet again. Aren't you satisfied?'

Oliver's mouth curved. 'No,' he said, realising as he did so that he was going further—much further—than he had ever intended. 'Not nearly,' he added, using her momentary confusion to cover the space between them. Then, ignoring the horrified look that entered her eyes as she realised what he intended, he cupped the tops of her arms with hard, determined hands. Concentrating on her lips, he pulled her towards him, and before she could turn her head away he covered her mouth with his.

Her mouth was soft and sweet—so sweet—and Oliver's head swam at the first taste of her lips. For all her opposition, he could feel the button-hard thrust of her nipples, taut against his chest, and although her hands came up to press him away her palms were hot through the thin cotton of his shirt.

Was she wearing a bra? he wondered. Probably one of those strapless, half-cupped items, that did little to contain the lush fullness of her breasts, he decided, resisting the impulse to rush things. He badly wanted to touch her breasts. He wanted to hold them and lift them, and feel those throbbing nipples against his palms, but for the present he contented himself with ravaging her mouth. He'd already had two chances with her, and he'd blown them both. He had no intention of blowing a third.

All the same, he didn't know what message she thought she was conveying, as her fingers curled and spread against his midriff. God, he was already as hard as a rock, and if she brushed her hips against his one more time he was going to explode.

Capturing her face between his palms, he tantalised her quivering tongue with his, and she uttered a helpless little moan that told him more about the way she was feeling than any helpless attempt to hold him off. Whatever she wanted to believe, she wanted him just as desperately as he wanted her. She wasn't fighting him, she was fighting her own feelings, and he felt an exultant sense of pride that he could do this to her. He had the feeling Robert had barely scratched the surface of her emotions, and the wild hunger she was feeling was as powerful as it was unfamiliar.

As his mouth continued its drugging assault on hers, Oliver let his hands slide from her cheeks, down the sides of her neck to her bare shoulders. As he bit softly at her lips, sucking the tip of her tongue into his mouth, his thumbs tipped the straps of her dress down over her arms. The loosened bodice revealed the creamy rise of her breasts, and he caught his breath as he glimpsed their swollen perfection.

He longed to peel the dress, and the lacy half-bra he had exposed, away from her, but as far as he knew, Mrs Neil could be in the kitchen, and liable to interrupt them at any time. He couldn't risk that kind of embarrassment, he thought ruefully, but when Fliss's tongue brushed sensuously against the roof of his mouth he was unbearably tempted. Who knew when—or even if—he would be allowed to see her again?

His hands moved down her back to her waist, his thumbs meeting across her flat stomach. She had a deliciously small waist, and the swell of her hips was both satisfying shapely and sensuous. He couldn't resist the urge to press her softness against the aching thrust of his sex, and he groaned at the pleasure even that small capitulation gave him. He could imagine how much more satisfying it would be without the frustrating barrier of their clothes, and his limbs ached at the thought.

He uttered another groan, and Fliss, who had seemed content to let him nibble at the silky skin below her ear, lifted her head, as if in enquiry.

Controlling himself with a supreme effort of willpower, Oliver lifted his head, too. 'Mrs Neil?' he asked, dreading her reply, but Fliss's eyes were dark and slumberous.

'No,' she answered, half blankly, shaking her head. 'She's not here. Her sister—she was ill, so——'

Her voice trailed away as her eyes focused on his dark face, and Oliver tensed himself once again to face her resistance. But, it didn't come. Instead, she lifted her hand and ran her palm over the already roughening skin of his jawline. A look of confusion crossed her face, as if she wasn't entirely sure of what she was doing, but then her gaze settled on his mouth and a purely sensual expression touched her lips.

With a tentative finger she traced the moulded line of his mouth, and although Oliver was tempted to bite that tantalising invader he restrained himself. He sensed it would be wise to let her make her own pace, a feeling that was reinforced when she reached up to brush his lips with her own.

'Kiss me,' she commanded huskily, when he didn't immediately respond to her tasting, and it was beyond his powers of reason to resist. Besides, it was the first time she had invited him to touch her, and he didn't need any further encouragement.

'Let's find somewhere more comfortable,' he said thickly, swinging her up into his arms, his mouth hot and urgent against her throat. And because he only knew where the kitchen was on the ground floor, he started up the stairs.

It was a simple matter to find Fliss's bedroom. Only two doors stood open on the first landing, and the first of them was obviously her father's. Oliver felt an unfamiliar twinge of guilt when he saw one of Matthew Hayton's clerical collars residing on the dressing-table, but he squashed the feeling of betrayal it made him feel. He couldn't afford to have a conscience, he told himself grimly. Consciences were for fools and cowards; he had learned that in the jungles of South-east Asia, too.

Fliss's room was predictably feminine. Although he only gave it a cursory glance, his gaze was charmed by the lace-trimmed curtains at the open windows, and the assortment of bears and other soft toys that adorned the window seat. The walls were hung with a creamy striped paper, and the bed was gratifyingly large and quilted in a matching fabric.

The quilt was soft beneath his hand as he lowered Fliss onto the bed, and he spared a moment to kick off his boots before joining her on the soft coverlet. 'Beautiful,' he said huskily, cradling her slightly flushed face between his palms. 'You're beautiful. But you know that, don't you? God, you're the most beautiful creature I've ever seen.'

Fliss licked her upper lip, and Oliver gave in to the urge to do the same. 'I—I'm not beautiful,' she got out breathily, and he could tell from the glazed expression in her eyes that she was no longer in control of either herself or her emotions. Either she was an amazing actress, or she was totally at the mercy of her sexual needs, and Oliver was pretty sure it was the latter. As before, he had the sensation of dealing with someone who was wholly inexperienced, and he wondered what Hastings was thinking of to neglect her so.

But he didn't want to think about Robert Hastings now. For the first time he could remember, he was in danger of forgetting his own identity here, and while the hazards of that were apparent, he could no more have resisted his urges than she could.

He wanted her. God, how he wanted her! He couldn't wait to feel her slick muscles enfold him, and if that was a painful admission for someone like him to make, then so be it.

Covering her face with hot, insistent kisses, he allowed his hands to do what they had wanted to do for what seemed like forever. With the utmost care, he drew the folds of her bodice down to her waist, and then unclipped the frivolous bra.

Her breasts were every bit as full and luscious as he had imagined, the nipples knotted and distended, an irresistible invitation to his lips. Controlling his hunger with some difficulty, he lowered his head and took one of the dark, swollen areolae into his mouth, sucking on it so strongly that Fliss moaned and clutched his head. Her nails raked his scalp, and her fingers tangled in his hair. But she was totally unaware of it, arching helplessly against the pillows.

Not until he had tasted both breasts did he give in to the hands that were now tearing at his collar. With a skill learned in too many beds, he tore his shirt open, almost ripping off the buttons in his haste to shed his clothes. But it was worth the haste to feel her body against his, to see the fine hair that arrowed down his chest dark against her skin.

But it wasn't enough, not nearly enough. He had to see the rest of her, too, and propping himself up on his elbows, he tugged the dress down to her ankles. He thought he might have torn it. There was an ominous pause before the material gave way. But he tossed the garment on to the floor without contrition. He'd buy her a dozen new dresses, if only she'd let him.

She was wearing lacy briefs that matched the bra he had discarded earlier, but that was all. Her glorious legs were bare, and a delicious cluster of honey-coloured curls was visible through the silk.

Oliver was trembling. He knew it, and he knew why. He could hardly contain himself as he bent his head and pressed his face against that silky mound. His own erection was straining for release, and the scent of her arousal was like nectar to his senses.

She uttered a sound—it might have been a protest, he couldn't be sure—but she lifted her hips obediently when he tugged the briefs away. She even parted her legs to facilitate his efforts, apparently unaware of the provocation of her actions.

But Oliver was aware of it; aware, too, that if he didn't touch her soon he was going to disgrace himself completely. Even so, he couldn't resist the opportunity to put his hand where her briefs had been, cupping her mound possessively, and finding the damp core of her with his finger.

She flinched when he touched her, and for a moment he was afraid she was going to prevent him from going on. Her hands came to cover his, as if in some kind of belated protest, but when he eased his finger inside her, her hands fell away.

'Oh, God,' she moaned, giving voice to her emotions for the first time since he had brought her upstairs, and she shuddered half convulsively as he prevented her from pressing her legs together again.

'Just take it easy,' he told her softly, even though he was cursing under his breath because the button at his waistband refused to open. But at last the button gave way, and he released his aching sex, kicking the jeans away with an impatience born of necessity.

Yet, when he saw her eyes were closed, conversely he held back. Even though his needs were paramount, it was important that she should look at him; that she should know who had brought her to such a state of abandonment. For she was abandoned lying there, her limbs splayed, her hair coming loose from its braid and tumbling about her shoulders. She was the epitome of everything he had ever wanted in a woman, and he wanted her to look at him and know she wanted him, too.

Taking one of her hands, he brought it to him, steeling himself not to lose control as he wrapped her fingers about him. The feeling was unimaginable, the desire to move against her almost irresistible. But he forced himself to watch her face and not the erotic movements of his body.

And her eyes opened, almost immediately. She blinked for a moment, and then looked down at the point where they were joined, and caught her breath.

'You're—so big,' she breathed, half withdrawing her hand, but then seeming to change her mind again. 'Oliver——'

'So you know it's me,' he said huskily, and she gave a jerky nod.

'I know,' she whispered, lifting her free hand to his face. 'Do you want to kiss me?'

'I'm afraid I'm going to have to do much more than that,' Oliver uttered on a breathy sigh. 'Oh, Fliss—I can't wait any longer. I've got to be inside you...'

# CHAPTER NINE

'DID you type up those notes I gave you, Felicity?'

Matthew Hayton ran restless fingers through the pile of papers on his daughter's desk, succeeding in sending most of them fluttering to the floor. It wasn't often Felicity let him down, but this morning she was just sitting staring at her typewriter, making no effort to transcribe the handwritten manuscript he had left with her the night before.

Fliss blinked, and forced herself to attend to what her father was saying. 'I beg your——'

'The notes,' said the Reverend patiently. 'You remember? I gave you the folder last evening. Did you do them already?'

'What? Oh, no.' Fliss felt her cheeks deepen with colour. 'I'm sorry.'

Her father frowned. 'Are you ill, Felicity?' he asked, with some concern, laying a cool hand against her temple. 'Heavens, you're hot! Are you sure you're all right?'

'I'm fine, Daddy.' Fliss made a concerted effort to gather her thoughts, and rescued the file of notes from the bottom of the pile. 'Um—here they are. Do you want them?'

'Not if they're not typed,' replied her father, containing his frustration. 'But as you know, the bishop's coming to lunch, and I had hoped to show him what I was doing.'

Fliss sighed apologetically. 'I'll do them right away——'

'No, that won't be necessary.' Matthew Hayton patted her shoulder reassuringly. 'Whatever you say, I can see that you're not feeling on top form this morning. I'll just show him my notes, if he's interested. If he can't read my writing—well, I'll worry about that if it happens, hmm?'

'Oh, Daddy!'

Fliss felt terrible. And not just because she had let her father down. For heaven's sake, on a scale of one to ten, not typing the notes had to figure fairly low on the list. But, being unfaithful to Robert, making love with Oliver Lynch in her *own* bed—that was betrayal of a totally different kind.

God! How could she have been so foolish? She should never have invited him into the house. She'd known what he wanted, what he was doing there. She wasn't a fool—well, she hadn't thought so before. But to let him touch her, to let him make love to her, to give him that kind of hold over her—that was really stupid.

Yet, if she was honest—and Fliss generally was—she had to admit she had never shown a great deal of common sense where Oliver Lynch was concerned. When she was with him, she seemed to lose what little composure she had, and the fact that he had no respect for her or her position as Robert's fiancée seemed to show a lack of judgement on her part rather than his.

The awful thing was, she had always thought herself such a controlled individual until he came along. Her father, especially, would never have recognised his emotionally restrained daughter in the wild-eyed wanton Oliver Lynch had tumbled on her bed. Even now, it was hard to imagine herself as she had been then, and only the prickling of her breasts and a pulse beating in an unmentionable part of her anatomy when she reviewed what had happened convinced her it was real.

In some ways, it still seemed like a dream. Had she really let Oliver Lynch do that to her? No matter how often she thought about it, it seemed incredible that she had actually participated in her own downfall. After holding Robert off all these months, why had she let a man she barely knew make love to her?

The answer eluded her, though in her heart of hearts she knew it had something to do with the fact that no matter how she might despise herself for it, she was attracted to Oliver Lynch, just as he had said.

It would certainly explain why she had always been so nervous around him. Had she always sensed he could be dangerous to her? Had she been afraid even then he might expose her relationship with Robert for what it was?

But no. Whatever perverse fascination she might have for the other man, she *loved* Robert. She didn't love Oliver Lynch. She despised him. Despised him and herself for creating such a ghastly situation.

Yet, at the time, she hadn't cared about the consequences. She had been so caught up in her own emotions, she hadn't thought about the damage she was doing. All that had seemed important was that Oliver should go on kissing her, and touching her, and inciting her wilful body to even greater heights of passion, making her practically beg him to satisfy her needs.

And he had, she thought unwillingly, recalling the sleek thrust of his powerful body with a sudden weakness. Dear God, he had driven her nearly wild with excitement, taking her to the edge of madness so many times that, when she finally tipped over the brink, the sensations she had experienced were out of this world.

She had clutched him then, her nails digging into his shoulders, uttering little incoherent protestations that he seemed to find absurdly erotic. He'd encouraged her to voice her feelings, feeding on the moist sweetness of her lips. And when her muscles had convulsed he'd groaned, too, spilling his seed inside her.

It was no dream, she thought now, remembering how she had felt when she had awakened to find him gone. Even without her clothes strewn about the room, and the feeling of lethargy that had gripped her, she had known it had really happened. Oliver's scent was still on her sheets, even if he'd abandoned her.

She closed her eyes for a moment as she recalled how quickly delight had turned to disillusion. The marvellous feeling of well-being she had had when she awakened had only lasted as long as it took her to remember what she'd done. The fact that Oliver wasn't there, that he had left her as soon as he'd got what he came for, had made everything seem so sordid. Had he guessed that Robert had never made love to her? Had he gloried in her inexperience because it had signalled Robert's defeat?

She'd wanted to die then. She'd wanted to pull the covers over her head and never come out again. She hadn't even got the consolation of knowing he'd used a contraceptive. He'd asked her if she wanted him to, but she'd been so desperate for him to take her, she'd only shaken her head.

God, she had been so stupid! She had known he was still involved with Rose Chen, that he was unlikely to do anything to jeopardise their relationship, yet she had surrendered to his demands like a foolish virgin. To him, it had meant nothing. For some reason, she had intrigued him, and it had amused him to prove to her—and to himself—that he could do it. He didn't care who he hurt in the process. Just as long as he wasn't disappointed.

It had been her father's voice, as he chatted with Mr Hood before coming into the house, that had forced Fliss to take stock of the situation. She couldn't have her father see this room and guess what had been going on. She couldn't put that kind of burden on him. It was her problem, and she would have to deal with it, in whatever way she could.

So, by the time he came in, her tearstained cheeks were washed, her hair was brushed, and the dress Oliver had torn as he ripped it off her was hidden at the bottom of her wardrobe. Another dress had taken its place and, as she had expected, her father didn't notice any change in her appearance.

However, that was yesterday. After a virtually sleepless night, today Fliss was less able to hide her feelings. She had the feeling she was suffering a delayed case of shock, and the knowledge that she'd be seeing Robert in a few hours was making it difficult to concentrate on her work. She'd forgotten all about her father's notes, and she hastily scanned her appearance, half afraid she might have forgotten to put on her shoes or button her shirt.

'Um—you and Robert haven't fallen out, have you?' her father asked suddenly, coming back into the room with the file of notes still in his hand. 'I mean, I don't want to pry or anything, but with Lynch turning up again yesterday, I did wonder if it had caused a problem.'

'Oh—no.' Fliss managed to sound amazingly casual. She hadn't had to tell her father about Oliver's visit. Mr Hood had done that for her, and somehow she had put him off without an adequate explanation. She'd let him think Oliver had been hoping to see him, and if her conscience had troubled her on that score, it had seemed such a minor sin compared to the others she had committed.

'You didn't see Robert last night,' the Reverend pointed out now, and Fliss made a display of putting a carbon between two sheets of typing paper to avoid having to look at him.

'I told you: Rob was staying in London last night. There was some sort of meeting at the office this morning, and he wanted to be there early. You know Mr

Hastings used to stay up in town sometimes, when he was involved in meetings.'

'You also told me that Robert was complaining about not being involved in the running of the company,' replied her father mildly. 'There's nothing you're not telling me, is there, Felicity? Hastings hasn't got himself into some sort of mess?'

Fliss gasped, and now looked at her father. 'Mess?' she echoed. 'What kind of mess?'

Matthew Hayton shrugged. 'You tell me.' He paused. 'I just got a feeling—when I was talking to Lynch, the other day—that he knew something I didn't.' He shook his head. 'I'm probably imagining things. But with him coming to see me yesterday...'

Fliss's lips tightened. 'It was only a courtesy call, Daddy,' she exclaimed, inwardly cringing at the absurdity of her words. There had been nothing courteous about Oliver Lynch's behaviour. 'If he'd had anything—important—to talk to you about, he'd have stayed, wouldn't he?'

'Perhaps.' Her father frowned. 'Yes, you're probably right. But if he calls again, do try and detain him. I enjoyed our conversation. He's an interesting man.'

Fliss made some guarded rejoinder, and thankfully her father didn't pursue the subject. With the bishop coming for lunch, he had things to prepare, and with some relief she abandoned the typing and escaped to the garden, and the undemanding task of weeding.

Robert arrived in the late afternoon. Fliss was in the kitchen when she heard a man's voice in the hall, and for a moment her knees turned to jelly. It wasn't that Robert's voice was anything like Oliver's, but she hadn't been expecting him until the evening. He was supposedly coming to take her to an art exhibition in Market Risborough, and his arrival now, some two or three hours before time was disturbing.

'It's only Mr Hastings,' said Mrs Neil, noticing how she had lost colour, and Fliss thought how ineffectual she was at hiding her feelings. But she couldn't help wondering if Oliver had been at the London meeting, and what he had said to her fiancé.

'I know,' she said now, making a pretence of checking her hair to give herself time to compose herself. After all, she had conducted herself perfectly naturally while the bishop was here. And he should have been far more intimidating than the man she was going to marry.

To her relief, her father was with Robert when she joined them in the sitting-room. It was a little late for tea, but Matthew Hayton was offering his guest a glass of sherry. 'I'm afraid we don't keep any spirits in the house,' he was saying, and Fliss wondered what had happened to make Robert need stronger fortification.

'Thanks,' Robert responded, and although he saw Fliss in the doorway he swallowed the contents of his glass in a single gulp before greeting her.

'Ah, there you are, my dear,' her father observed, with an evident effort. 'Robert's here.'

'Yes. So I see.' Fliss managed to sound suitably surprised. 'Is—er—is something wrong?'

'What could be wrong?' asked Robert harshly, handing his glass to the Reverend in a mute appeal for a refill. He came towards her, and before she could guess his intention he had jerked her towards him and bestowed a wet, sherry-scented kiss on her mouth. 'I just couldn't wait to see you, that's all.'

Fliss's eyes sought her father's over Robert's shoulder, begging his indulgence, and although he would have obviously preferred to leave them to it Matthew Hayton poured his guest another sherry.

'Robert,' he said peremptorily, holding out the glass, and the younger man was forced to release Fliss to take it.

'Did—did you go to your meeting?' she asked warily, aware that Robert's behaviour was not typical. Something had happened. She was certain. But whether it was to do with her, she couldn't be sure.

'Oh, yes,' said Robert now. 'Yes, I went. It was most—enlightening.'

Fliss's stomach tightened. 'Really?'

'Yes, really.' Robert finished his second sherry, looked as if he might ask for a third, and then seemed to think better of it. He took a steadying breath. 'I've been recruited to the board.'

Fliss caught her breath. 'Oh! Oh, Rob—that's wonderful!'

'Is it?' His expression was sardonic.

'Well, isn't it?' She licked her lips. 'I—I thought that was what you wanted.'

'Yes. So did I.' Robert's lips twisted. 'Funny how wrong you can be.'

Fliss looked at her father, her own confusion plain, and clearing his throat, the older man stepped forward to take the empty glass. 'Um—does this mean you're going to be running the London end of the business from now on, my boy?'

Robert frowned. 'I'm not sure. I suppose I could be.'

'Oh, Rob!' Fliss's relief that her fiancé hadn't come here to accuse her of betraying him with Oliver Lynch made her more effusive than she might otherwise have been. 'Rose Chen must have great confidence in you.'

'Mmm.' Robert didn't sound as if that news filled him with delight. 'At least that bastard Lynch wasn't at the meeting. According to Rose, he's not involved in the operation.'

'No?' Fliss swallowed.

'No.' Robert's mouth hardened. 'He's just a hanger-on, as I always thought. But if he thinks he's got Rose in his pocket, he's way off base, as they say in his country.'

For the first time since Fliss had entered the room, Robert smiled, but it was not a pleasant expression. Whatever had happened in London, it was Robert who considered he had got the better of the other man. And, although Fliss couldn't suppress a totally unnecessary twinge of concern on Oliver's behalf, she was relieved that she hadn't been involved.

'I didn't get that impression,' Matthew Hayton remarked suddenly, and Fliss, who had been congratulating herself that the danger was over for the moment, cast him an anxious look. 'Lynch,' went on her father, when Robert looked blank. 'He didn't strike me as a—what was it you said? A hanger-on? I found him a very intelligent human being. Did you know, for instance, that he studied law when he was younger? I'd say he'd make a very fine student.' He paused. 'I should add that he didn't volunteer this information to impress me. I questioned him about his education, and he was obliged to admit that he had abandoned his career to join the army. He served in Vietnam, you know. An experience which damaged quite a number of young men, I believe.'

Robert's smile had disappeared now, and he looked resentfully at the older man. 'Are you saying that's an excuse for living off my sister,' he demanded.

'No.' Matthew Hayton drew himself up to his full height. At a little under six feet, he was still a couple of inches shorter than Robert, but his presence was impressive. 'I'm saying that someone who's lived a fairly comfortable existence all his life shouldn't jump to totally unfounded conclusions.'

'Now, look here——'

'Oh, please.' Fliss put herself between the two men, realising, if Robert didn't, that he was in danger of alienating her father completely. Besides, she had no wish to have to explain why Oliver had come here a second time, not unless it was absolutely necessary, of course. 'Does it matter what either of you thinks of him? As you've just said, Rob, he's not involved. Let's leave it at that.'

Robert looked as if he would have liked to continue the argument, but Fliss's intervention had reminded him of his obligations, and he had no wish to fall out with his future father-in-law. 'Suits me,' he said, albeit a little off-handedly, and the Reverend inclined his head in a gesture of acceptance.

'I'd better go and prepare for choir practice,' he said, addressing himself to no one in particular, and Fliss let her breath escape on a thankful sigh as he departed the room.

As soon as he had gone, Robert reached for her again, but Fliss managed to evade his possessive hands, and went to open the french doors into the garden. It was probably her, but the room seemed airless suddenly, and she couldn't wait to get outside. She stepped out on to the terrace, knowing Robert would follow her, and put the width of the wicker garden table between them, before he could approach her again.

'So,' she said, hurrying into speech so he wouldn't notice her nervousness, 'what happened?'

Robert frowned. 'What do you mean?' he asked, evidently diverted, as she had hoped.

'Well—you didn't seem exactly thrilled with the new arrangement when you arrived,' she pointed out carefully. 'Did Rose Chen give you a hard time?'

Robert hunched his shoulders, pushing his hands into the pockets of his jacket. He was still wearing the navy business suit he had worn at the meeting, and although he had unloosened his collar, he still looked hotter than she felt.

'Rose is OK,' he said, after a moment, and Fliss, who had been expecting anything but this, widened her eyes.

'She is?'

'Well——' Robert gave a careless shrug, no doubt remembering the invective he had previously used to describe his half-sister. 'I suppose she is family, whether I like it or not.'

Fliss hid her amazement. 'I see.'

'I know what you're thinking. You're thinking that because I've been invited to join the board, I've had a change of heart.'

'Well——'

'Well, that's not it.' Robert flushed. 'You don't understand. It's not as—simple—as I thought. Rose has had a pretty tough time since my father died, and it's up to us—my mother and me—to take some of that burden from her.'

'Oh.' Fliss hoped she didn't sound as horrified as she felt. But the idea of Rose Chen being accepted as part of Robert's 'family'; of her staying at the Grange, as a welcome visitor; of her becoming not just a business partner but his 'sister', filled her with alarm. For Rose Chen, she read Oliver Lynch, and the thought of seeing him again, maybe even on a regular basis if Rose Chen had her way, was unthinkable.

'What's wrong?'

Robert asked the question now, and Fliss realised that once again she was letting her emotions show. 'N-nothing,' she stammered, desperate to escape a prolonged postmortem of her feelings. 'I'm just surprised, that's all. I didn't think you liked her.'

Robert hesitated. Then, 'I don't,' he admitted, and she realised that what he had said before had been just self-justification. 'But I've got to work with her, Fliss. She holds the purse-strings. And what does it matter where the money comes from, as long as there's plenty of it?'

Fliss looked at him curiously now. 'What's that supposed to mean?' she asked, and Robert's eyes flickered uneasily.

'Nothing,' he said impatiently, and his momentary show of conscience might never have been. 'It means nothing. I was only thinking aloud, that's all. Now, why don't we drive into Market Risborough and get something to eat there, before going to the exhibition?'

Fliss shrugged. 'All right.'

'Good.' Robert looked at her expectantly. 'Well? Aren't you going to get ready?'

'Now?' Fliss stared at him in some confusion. 'But——' She looked at his suit which was creased from his journey. 'Aren't you going to get changed?'

'No, I don't think I will.' A faint trace of colour entered Robert's fair cheeks as he made his excuses. 'I—er—I can't be bothered to go back home just now.' He glanced down at his appearance. 'I'll do, won't I?'

What could she say? Fliss made a helpless gesture, and moved towards the house again. 'But—won't your mother expect to see you, to talk to you, to hear what happened?' she asked finally, and Robert sighed.

'My mother was at the meeting,' he said flatly. 'I dropped her at the Grange on my way here.' His lips thinned. 'Now, are we going out or aren't we? I'd really like to know.'

# CHAPTER TEN

'AND you think he's been told what's going on?' Colonel Lightfoot sounded thoughtful. 'If it's true, isn't Rose taking a God-awful risk?'

'That depends.' Oliver considered the options. 'She could have been lying all along, of course. She and Robert could both have been playing a double game, but I don't think Hastings is clever enough for that. I think this is a calculated move on Rose's part.' He paused. 'What I've yet to discover is why. She's not the type to take chances. Not when there's so much at stake.'

The colonel made a sound of assent. 'So, what's your guess?'

Oliver shrugged, shifting the phone to his other ear. 'I don't have one. Not one I'd care to air yet, anyway. I'll wait and see what transpires. I've told Rose I want to return to Hong Kong by the end of next week, so——'

'What the hell did you do that for?' The colonel erupted into a frustrated tirade. 'For God's sake, man, do you want to lose whatever ground you've gained?'

'No.' Oliver kept his tone mild with an effort. It would be all too easy to vent his feelings in his present frame of mind, but he had no intention of giving Lightfoot another goad to lash him with. 'It's because I don't want Rose to get suspicious of me that I'm putting a deadline on the time I stay here. Don't let's forget, I'm supposed to be involved in deals of my own. What kind of jerk would I seem if I was prepared to hang about indefinitely? As far as she knows, I'm just wasting my time here. Who knows? Maybe it'll persuade her to offer me a reason to stay on.'

'Huh.' The colonel didn't sound convinced. If there was any merit in the idea, he wasn't about to admit it. 'Well, I hope you're right.'

'Yeah. So do I,' drawled Oliver evenly, aware that Colonel Lightfoot would very likely burst a blood vessel if he found out how his supposedly professional operative had been spending his time. 'I'll call you again, when I've got something to report.'

'In two days, Lynch,' said Colonel Lightfoot pedantically, but Oliver wasn't listening. He put down his receiver without acknowledging the order.

However, with the connection broken, and the rest of the day at his disposal, Oliver was less inclined to be arrogant. Whatever he'd told the colonel, his association with Rose Chen had never been at a lower ebb. Although Rose didn't know it, his infatuation with Fliss Hayton was the reason for the deterioration in their relationship, and after the row they had had last evening it was highly unlikely that she'd be offering him any kind of inducement to stay.

The knowledge angered him. He wasn't used to any kind of interference in his professional activities. Even his affair with Rose Chen had been carefully orchestrated, and at no time had he ever felt out of touch with his objective. He had been doing a good job, making good progress, and now he was allowing his feelings for Fliss to foul up not just his job, but his life.

He didn't like it. He liked what he'd done even less. What was wrong with him, for God's sake? Was he having some kind of mid-life crisis slap damn in the middle of a surveillance operation? And what would old Archie think if he told him he couldn't go on because he was emotionally involved with one of the principals?

He groaned. He could imagine what Archie would say all right, and it wouldn't be complimentary. And who could blame him? Dammit, he wasn't just acting out of line, he was acting out of character. He didn't get emotionally involved with women—any women. But least of all a vicar's daughter, for Pete's sake!

But he had—and that was what was eating him up. Cheating on Hastings didn't bother him. He'd dismissed the arguments on that days ago. He'd told himself then, he couldn't afford to have a conscience. In his line of work, a man used any means in his power to gain the upper hand, and if it meant compromising his own morals then so be it. It was Fliss who was causing him to question his motives—because he knew that, whatever excuses he might give himself, what he'd done he'd done for his own gratification and nothing else.

Which was why he'd been in such a filthy mood when he'd got back from Sutton Magna the day before. It wasn't just the risks he'd taken with his relationship with Rose Chen, though God knew, if she was as ruthless as her father had been, it might not just be his job he was putting in jeopardy. It was the realisation that he felt only contempt for his own actions. Fliss had trusted him, and look how he had repaid her.

And for once, the argument that he was only doing a job didn't hold any water. Seducing Hastings' fiancée had not been part of his brief, and the memory of how he had used her own inexperience against her filled him with shame. It was no consolation that what had happened had disturbed him equally as much as it had disturbed her. She didn't know it was the first time in his life he had actually lost control of his emotions. She probably thought he had used her, as he had used so many other women before, and she'd never forgive him for that.

But did he want her to forgive him? Wasn't it better, for both of them, if she continued to regard him as the bastard he was? He didn't need her understanding. He wanted no distractions to what he was being paid to do.

Nevertheless it had been a salutary lesson in how not to behave. Remembering how he had even failed to protect her from his lust only added to his sense of self-disgust. He wasn't a boy, for God's sake. He should have been capable of restraining himself long enough to take the usual precautions. But he hadn't. His need to fuse his body with hers had blinded him to all normal considerations, and even now, in the midst of his soul-searching, he could feel himself hardening at the thought.

God! He swore angrily. The trouble was, what had happened hadn't achieved the result he'd expected. No matter how crazy he knew it to be, once had simply not been enough. The way he felt at the moment, he doubted a lifetime would be long enough to slake the hunger Fliss had aroused in him. How the hell was he supposed to concentrate on his own safety, when all he could think about was how he could contrive to see her again?

But he mustn't see her again, he told himself savagely. For her sake, as well as his own. Whatever fleeting satisfaction they had shared, she was still going to marry Hastings. And, looking at it objectively, if he had alerted her to the sensuality of her nature, then her fiancé ought to thank him. He had the feeling Robert was somewhat short on sensitivity.

He snorted suddenly. Who was he kidding? His lips twisted. God, was he really that arrogant? Was he actually making a case for his own redemption, when what he should really be doing was acknowledging that the thought of Fliss in the other man's arms was tearing him to pieces? She had been his, dammit. And the truth, if he was man enough to admit it, was that he wanted more from her than just a hasty tumble in the sheets.

But that way lay madness, and defeat. However he might kick against it, Fliss Hayton was not for him. It had been an enlightening experience, but that was all. He had to get the whole thing into perspective and start concentrating on the real reason he was here.

Which meant getting back into Rose Chen's good graces. If he wasn't careful Hastings would succeed in poisoning her mind against him, too, and he couldn't allow that. He had come too far, sacrificed too much. He wasn't going to lose out now.

'But who are these people, Rob? And why do I have to meet them? If it's business——'

'You met my father's business associates from time to time,' Robert interrupted her shortly, and Fliss, who had been hoping to avoid any further involvement with either Oliver or Rose Chen, wanted to scream.

'Even so——'

'Look: it's what I want,' her fiancé broke in again. 'You ought to be glad I'm being involved in the business at last. At least I know what's going on now. And— well, these people like to know who they're dealing with.'

'What people?' Fliss gazed at him. 'And if you wanted to entertain them, why haven't you invited them to the Grange?'

'So many questions!' Robert strode impatiently around the sitting-room at the vicarage. 'What's the matter? Don't you trust me enough to spend the night with me?' His lips curled. 'No, I'll rephrase that. Don't you trust me to book you a room of your own at the hotel?'

'Oh, Rob——'

'What? What is it with you, Fliss? Don't you want to support me in this? Can't you see that it's what I've got to do if we ever hope to have a life of our own?'

Fliss gazed at him anxiously. Was it just her own guilt feeding her uncertainties, or were Robert's explanations growing progressively more ambiguous? Ever since he had told her he had joined the board of Hastings', he had seemed to have a meaning deeper than the actual words he used.

For a while she had entertained the possibility that somehow he had found out about her and Oliver, and this was his way of telling her. But it was several days since the traumatic events of that morning, and, knowing Robert as she did, she couldn't believe he would conceal his feelings for so long. Besides, it was becoming increasingly obvious that it wasn't her behaviour that was on his mind, and this invitation to attend a private dinner party in London was obviously important to him.

But as soon as he had told her that Rose Chen would be there, Fliss had been desperate to avoid the confrontation. Rose Chen meant Oliver, and she didn't think she could face him again. Not now, not yet. Not until she had had time to recover a little of the pride he had so cruelly robbed her of.

'So?' Robert prompted now, and Fliss realised she had spent far too long mulling over her own situation. He was looking at her now with scarcely concealed irritation, and if she wasn't careful she would give him reason for questioning her motives.

'I don't know if I can,' she mumbled, pulling the dead stem of a carnation out of a vase, and folding it up between her fingers. It was slimy, and she pulled a face, before adding lamely, 'Daddy may need me.'

'*I* need you,' retorted Robert harshly. 'Come on, Fliss. If we're ever going to make a go of our relationship you've got to start deciding where your priorities are.'

Fliss bit her lip. She knew that. She knew she was being unforgivably selfish. But the trouble was, she didn't know what her priorities were any longer. She'd thought she did. She'd thought that marrying Robert would give her everything she had ever wanted from her life, but now she was not so sure.

Of course, she was being foolish. Ridiculously foolish in the circumstances. It wasn't as if she wanted to marry anyone else, after all. She wasn't stupid enough to believe that she had any future with Oliver Lynch. Even if he'd wanted it, she had more sense than to ally herself to a man who treated her sex with so little respect.

She wondered if he'd told Rose Chen what he'd done. She doubted it, remembering how possessive the Chinese woman had been, but it was always possible. She'd read it was how some people kept their relationships alive. Though, judging how fiery Rose Chen's response to him had been, she doubted they needed any artificial stimulant. She felt sick every time she pictured them together, and no amount of self-analysis could alter the fact that she hated them both in equal measure.

'All right,' she said now, realising that whatever their future might hold, she couldn't let Robert down. 'But I hope you know what you're doing.'

'What's that supposed to mean?'

Robert's response was instantly defensive, and Fliss sighed. 'Nothing,' she said. 'I'm just not sure that working with—with that woman is making you happy.'

'Happy?' Robert gave her an odd look. 'What's "happy" got to do with anything? She's going to make me rich. That's what matters, isn't it?'

Fliss wasn't so sure. She was very much afraid that Robert was willing to do almost anything to sustain his position in the company. From the beginning his main concern had been that he shouldn't get his fair share of the business, and now that Rose Chen had solicited his help he seemed desperate to justify her acceptance.

Still, as she got ready to leave the following afternoon, Fliss decided there was no point in worrying about it. What could Rose make him do, for heaven's sake? Falsify records? Condone the sale of some item of doubtful provenance? She had no doubt it happened, and not just with Hastings'; the antiques business was as open to fraud as any other. And the fact that James Hastings had lived in comparative luxury all his life seemed to point to the fact that he had either been amazingly fortunate or amazingly clever. Either way, Fliss would have believed anything of that cold, unfeeling man. He had

had no heart, just a superficial charm—which she supposed was a fair description of his eldest daughter, too.

Her father was waiting to bid her farewell. He smiled his approval as she came down the stairs, but she sensed he wasn't entirely happy with the arrangements. He thought it very remiss of Robert to expect her to drop everything and travel up to London with him at a moment's notice, and although she had had slightly longer than that, Fliss could understand his feelings.

'You will phone after you're installed at the hotel, won't you?' he said, as they heard Robert's car pull up outside. 'And if you have any problem—any problem at all—don't hesitate to let me know.'

'I'm only going to be away one night, Daddy.' Fliss tried to make light of it. 'And I'm sure you'd rather Rob didn't drive home if he's going to be drinking.'

'Of course, of course.' Matthew Hayton pushed his hands into the pockets of his worn corduroy trousers and regarded her ruefully. 'I'm just an old worry-wart, that's all.'

'Well, I'm sure there's no need.' Fliss bit her lip. 'I'm only going to be with Rob, you know. You trust him, don't you?'

'I suppose so.' Her father looked a little discomfited now. He paused, and then added, 'I've just had the feeling lately that you've been having—well—second thoughts about him yourself.'

Fliss caught her breath. 'About Rob?'

'I actually wondered if Oliver was to blame,' her father continued steadily. 'Whether he'd made you a little—restless.' He shrugged, as Fliss struggled to control her colour. 'It was just a thought.'

'No.' The doorbell rang, and Fliss glanced half furtively towards it. 'I mean—no, I'm not having second thoughts, Daddy. And—and definitely not about Oliver Lynch!'

'OK.' Her father made a dismissing movement with his shoulders as the doorbell rang again. 'You'd better answer that. Patience has never been Robert's strong point.'

Fliss stared at him, unmoving, for another few seconds. She'd known that Robert and her father had had their differences in the past, but she'd never realised how deep-rooted they were. When had Matthew Hayton begun to actively dislike her fiancé? And where had he got the notion that her relationship with Oliver might be more or less than it appeared?

The bell rang for a third time, and the Reverend shook his head. 'The door,' he prompted, and with a feeling of bemusement Fliss went to answer it.

Robert was predictably terse. 'Doesn't this bell work or something?' he demanded, before he saw Fliss's father behind her in the hallway. He coloured. 'I thought it must be out of order,' he added, for the older man's benefit. 'I've rung it half a dozen times.'

'Three actually,' corrected Matthew Hayton evenly, and then turned to give his daughter a kiss. 'Now, remember what I said,' he murmured, giving her cheek an affectionate pat. Then, to Robert, 'Drive carefully.'

Robert stowed Fliss's holdall and the suit carrier containing her dress, into the back of the car, and then got into the seat beside her. He was very tense; she could feel it. And she didn't think it was just her father's attitude that had sparked his temper, though he chose to pretend it was.

'Dammit, you'd think I was a schoolboy, the way he talks to me,' he complained angrily, as they headed for the motorway. 'And what was all that about you remembering what he'd said? Is he afraid I'm going to jump you the minute I've got you to the hotel?'

Fliss sighed. 'Of course not.'

'Why "of course not"? Doesn't he think I've got it in me to seduce my own fiancée?'

'Rob!'

'Well, it's true.' Robert hunched his shoulders over the wheel, and Fliss guessed they were in for a fast ride to London. 'I know he doesn't approve of the arrangements, so don't pretend he does. Just wait until we're married. He won't be able to call the shots then.'

Fliss sighed again. 'Rob, he's not like that.'

'He's exactly like that.' With a swift depression of the accelerator Robert cut in front of a slow-moving wagon, causing it to break and blow its horn furiously. 'And you,' he muttered, giving the other man an uncomplimentary gesture. 'Bloody professional drivers! They think they own the road.'

'He was trying to keep a reasonable distance between him and the car in front,' said Fliss carefully. 'You closed the gap.'

'When I want instruction from you, I'll ask for it,' retorted Robert aggressively, opening his window, and throwing his elbow over the rim. 'I'm sick to death of people giving me orders. If you can't say anything pleasant, don't say anything at all.'

Fliss drew a deep breath, refusing to respond to his ill humour in kind. At times Robert *was* like a small boy, and this was one of them. She already had doubts about this evening, and his behaviour was only adding to her misgivings.

'Anyway, we've got to talk about other things,' he muttered, and, if it wasn't an apology, at least he didn't intend to sulk all the way to London. 'I may have to go to Hong Kong in a couple of months myself, and my mother thinks we should get married before I go.'

'What?'

Fliss turned a startled face towards him now, but Robert refused to look at her. 'Well, we were planning on getting married at Christmas, weren't we? If we bring it forward a couple of months, what does it matter?'

'We're talking about four months, at least,' exclaimed Fliss hotly, and then, realising she was panicking, she forced herself to calm down. 'If—if you do have to go to Hong Kong, then I think it would be more sensible if you got that out of the way before we got married. We could always postpone the wedding.' She despised herself for the relief she felt at the prospect. 'There's no urgency about it, is there?'

'Not for you, perhaps,' muttered Robert dourly. 'My God, I sometimes wonder if you've got a sexual urge in your body! Besides——' he took his eyes from the road for a moment to cast her a glowering look, and then had to brake fiercely to avoid another collision '—it's not an either-or situation,' he growled. 'You don't seem to understand. The reason we have to get married before I go to Hong Kong is simple. I don't know how long I'm going to have to stay there. I'm going to run the Hong Kong office. If it works out, it could be months; years, even. Naturally, you'll come with me. As my wife——'

'No!' Fliss was horrified. 'I—I—what about Daddy?'

'What about *Daddy*?' Robert was sardonic. 'You surely knew when we got married he'd have to manage on his own.'

'Well, yes, but——'

'But, what? But not with you in Hong Kong, hmm? Well, I can't say I'm particularly excited about the prospect myself. I'd always imagined I'd have charge of the London office, as I told you. But—well, Rose thinks I should take over the Far East operation for a while.' He grimaced. 'I guess I can see her point. If she involves me in every aspect of the business, there'll be no chance that I'll—that is——' He broke off abruptly, and Fliss sensed he was rephrasing what he had been going to say. 'Make a hash of it,' he went on eventually. 'I'll be fully equipped to understand what's going on.'

Fliss's breath escaped in a rush. 'And—and when do you expect us to get married?' she ventured, knowing even as she asked the question that his answer would mean nothing to her. She was here, and she was committed to spending this evening with him, but as far as marrying Robert was concerned her father was right: she was having second thoughts. Particularly if he thought he could rush her into it.

Robert's expression lightened. He evidently thought her enquiry meant he had convinced her. 'Oh, I don't know. Shall we say six weeks? I may have to fly out to Hong Kong in the meantime, but that should give you enough time to organise everything. After all,' he grinned, 'it's not as if we have to make an appointment to see the vicar and book the church, is it?'

Fliss said nothing. This was not the time to air her doubts with him. She wanted to discuss the matter with her father first, and if that was an indication of how her feelings towards Robert had changed, then so be it.

All the same, she was not unaware of the enormity of her decision. Until these last few weeks she had anticipated the prospect of her coming wedding with the usual expectancy of any young bride. If she had had any misgivings about their relationship, she had submerged them beneath the belief that what she was doing was right; that Robert loved her, and she loved him.

But James Hastings' death had changed a lot of things, not least her interpretation of Robert's character. Even without her unholy association with Oliver Lynch, she had learned things about her fiancé she had previously not known—or perhaps had ignored. He could be selfish and self-pitying; he could be rude and aggressive—even with her father; and he was also weak where money was concerned, willing to sacrifice his lofty principles, too, if his way of life was threatened.

And that was why she was hesitating, Fliss assured herself grimly. Not because of Oliver Lynch, or through

any hope that he cared anything about her. Her opinion
of him hadn't changed. She hated and despised him. But
she knew she'd never forget him—and that was the
hardest cut of all.

# CHAPTER ELEVEN

OLIVER accompanied Rose Chen to the club that evening with a curious feeling of detachment. Sitting in the back of the chauffeur-driven limousine, he was aware that he should have been in excellent spirits. After all, he had achieved all he had expected to achieve, and he should have felt elated. But he didn't. He felt cold, ambivalent; indifferent to the success he had contrived.

Which was some admission for a so-called professional to make, he thought wryly. He was actually anticipating the end of this mission with real relief. He had had enough of being Lightfoot's animal. He wanted to be in control of his own life again.

In a fit of nostalgia he had even spoken to his father the day before. The old man had sounded almost emotional over the transatlantic link, and when he'd heard that his son was coming home he'd been genuinely delighted. Oliver had been away for far too long, he said. Both he and his mother couldn't wait for him to settle again in Maple Falls.

Oliver hid a grimace. He didn't really know whether returning to Maple Falls was what he wanted. The truth was, he wanted something he couldn't have. Fliss had taught him there was more to life than death or glory, and a home, and family—even if he had to settle for second-best—had to be better than what he had now.

His only consolation was that Fliss wasn't involved in this rotten business. If she had already been married to Robert Hastings she would have been regarded as guilty by association. As it was, she had a chance to make her life again—even if it wasn't with the man she loved.

He supposed James Hastings' one redeeming feature had been his decision not to involve his son. Or perhaps Robert's free-wheeling lifestyle had saved him from corruption. Either way, James Hastings hadn't considered his son a suitable candidate for the organisation. Rose Chen had been a much more noteworthy advocate, and the fact that she was also his daughter must have lent the arrangement a certain piquancy.

Certainly Rose had proved herself a worthy successor, Oliver reflected now. No one in the London office questioned her orders, and that after only a few short weeks. Which might explain why her father had kept their relationship a secret from her. Had he been afraid she might supersede him? She was obviously less scrupulous, and ruthless to a fault.

She hadn't hesitated before telling her brother the facts of life. Although Oliver hadn't been present at the meeting, the fact that Robert was now involved in the decision-making process had proved that she had seen his ignorance as a danger. Rose worked on the premise that everyone was as self-seeking as herself. Oliver guessed Robert had been warned that threatening Rose was ultimately threatening himself.

In a way, Oliver pitied the younger man. He had looked pretty sick the last time he'd seen him at the office. If he had been as ignorant of what was going on as Oliver now suspected, it must have been a bitter pill to swallow. But weakness was no excuse for complicity.

From Oliver's point of view Robert's involvement was a fairly unimportant development. The computer disk he had copied, and which was presently in the hands of the Royal Mail, was a far more interesting coup. The names and figures it contained might have been meaningless to him, but they were no doubt invaluable to the relevant authorities. It was that which would give Lightfoot the information he needed, which would grant Oliver his freedom.

He sighed. If he had any doubts at all, they concerned the way he had acquired the disk. It had seemed almost too easy. And yet, remembering the things Rose had had on her mind that morning, was it really so surprising that she should have overlooked that one small detail?

The call, saying that the *Oriental Princess* had just docked after being escorted into the Pool of London by Her Majesty's Coastguard had caused the panic. The Chinese vessel, with its consignment of jade and porcelain, gold and Chinese carpets, had been involved in a collision with another vessel in Blackwall Reach, and the Customs and Excise people were showing an inordinate interest in its cargo.

Oliver had pitied the poor captain of the vessel. He knew that the last thing Rose wanted was anyone examining the cargo too closely. She didn't want anyone telling her that the items she was paying so highly to import were not the ancient artefacts she was declaring. The success of the operation depended on the fact that for years no one had suspected that someone who dealt in items that attracted such a swingeing duty could be involved in smuggling.

In consequence, Rose had rushed away to deal with the matter personally, leaving the disk she had been using in the computer. And, taking one of those chances that his life seemed to be composed of recently, Oliver had extracted the disk, carried it into one of the empty offices, and copied it. By the time Rose returned, it was safely back in the computer, and Oliver was somewhere else.

In any case, she trusted him, didn't she? Since he had convinced himself that Fliss was never going to forgive him—not just for taking advantage of her, but also for being involved in Robert's eventual arrest and conviction—he had expended a good deal of time and energy in convincing Rose their relationship hadn't changed. He had worked hard to suppress his real feelings. Why

shouldn't she trust him? So far as Rose was concerned
he was as ignorant of her real activities as he had ever
been. Which was probably why he was still around, he
reflected ruefully. Anyone who crossed Rose could expect
swift retribution, and if she'd suspected his real motives
he might well have returned home in a body bag.

Nevertheless, Rose was becoming increasingly arrogant, and it had been only a matter of time before she
took complete control of the operation. Her importance
to the company, and the fact of her relationship to James
Hastings, had given her an added advantage, and Oliver
doubted she would have allowed Robert to snap at her
heels for long.

Oliver gave an inward sigh. It was just as well he was
getting out. His own involvement with Fliss was threatening his objectivity. He was even feeling sorry for
Robert, poor bastard. He was weak and mercenary, no
doubt. But was that really grounds for complete
emasculation?

Still, for tonight, at least, he had no choice but to be
on his best behaviour. This dinner party was important
to Rose, and although he suspected the men they were
about to meet were the real criminals here, nothing could
alter the fact that Rose, and Robert—and Amanda
Hastings, too, he suspected—had been perfectly willing
to supply a market whose only traffic was in misery.

But meeting these men meant little to Oliver. He could
do nothing to stop them; not personally, at any rate. He
was not foolish enough to think he could be a hero. If
these men disappeared, others would take their place.
What Oliver—and Lightfoot—were trying to do was cut
off the trade at source.

'What are you thinking about, lover?'

Rose Chen's hand on his thigh reminded him of where
he was, and Oliver dragged his thoughts back to the
present. Until he could leave, until he could get on the
plane back to Hong Kong, he had to continue playing

his part. It wouldn't do to make her suspicious, even if the muscles of his thigh threatened to reject her possessive fingers.

'Home,' he said swiftly, and not altogether untruthfully. 'I shall miss you when I go back to Hong Kong.'

'Then we'll have to see if we can find you something to do here in London,' murmured Rose Chen softly. 'Did I tell you I'm sending Robert to Hong Kong? He and that—sweet—fiancée of his are going to have to bring their wedding forward. Robert wants to take her with him, naturally, and I don't think her father would approve of anything else.'

Oliver swallowed the instinctive retort that rose into his throat, and then said carefully, 'You're sending Robert to Hong Kong? Is that wise?'

Rose shrugged. 'It's—expeditious,' she replied, with a secret smile. 'I'll ask Suntong to keep an eye on him.'

'Mmm.' Oliver could hardly hide his anger. 'I've no doubt you will.'

'You're not jealous, are you, lover?'

Rose was watching him closely as she spoke, and Oliver could feel the beads of sweat fairly bursting to break out on his upper lip. But, 'Jealous?' he managed, with just the right inflection. 'Of Robert Hastings? Do me a favour.'

'Of his relationship with the Hayton woman,' inserted Rose impatiently. 'Don't tell me you haven't noticed her, because I won't believe you.'

Oliver made a supreme effort and forced a reminiscent smile. 'Oh,' he said, and, realising there was no point in being unnecessarily obtuse, his lips twisted. 'That.'

'Yes, that,' said Rose tensely. 'Did you sleep with her?'

'Rose!' Oliver gazed at her with wounded eyes, amazed at his own capacity for deceit. 'What do you take me for?'

'I take you for an oversexed animal who's had far too much time on his own lately,' declared Rose acidly. 'And don't look at me like that. I know I've been neglecting you. But that's going to change.'

'Is it?' Oliver couldn't believe his luck. Rose was so conceited, she actually believed *she* had been neglecting *him*, and not the other way about.

'Yes,' she said, lifting her hand and cupping his face with strong aggressive fingers. 'I'm thinking of making you my personal assistant. That way, you can stay in London, and I can keep an eye on you.'

'But I thought we were having dinner at the hotel,' Fliss protested, peering out of the grimy windows of the cab. The streets beyond the windows were unfamiliar to her, and, although it should still have been light, a lowering sky and the occasional patter of rain on the windscreen was heralding a wet evening.

'I don't believe I said where we were dining,' replied Robert impatiently. Then, taking a calming breath. 'Besides, I didn't make the arrangements. Rose chose the venue. Blame her if you're not happy.'

*Happy*!

Fliss pressed her shoulders back against the worn leather upholstery, wishing she had refused to come at all. If only she had known that Robert was going to spring this Hong Kong trip on her. If only she had realised how she really felt, before she'd got herself into this mess.

And there was still the prospect of meeting Oliver to face. How was she going to look at him, and talk to him, without being overwhelmingly aware of how he had last seen her? What had he thought, when he'd left her there among the tumbled bedclothes? Did he despise her now as much as she despised herself?

'What's the matter?' Robert had taken her silence for sulkiness and, shifting his position, he put his arm along the back of her seat. 'Did I tell you, you look stunning?' he asked, deliberately changing tactics. 'Wait until my mother sees you. She's always asking me what I see in you. Well, now she's going to know.'

Fliss stiffened, refusing to be disarmed by his attempts at flattery. As a matter of fact she had decided she disliked her dress violently. Its amber folds were too revealing, and the taffeta was too rich.

In fact, she knew the dress suited her very well. Too well for her to hope to remain unnoticed. But the situation had changed since she had chosen the dress. Then, she had had some crazy notion of making Oliver jealous, of showing him what he'd lost. She'd wanted him to see how unimportant he was to her. Now, all she wanted was for the evening to be over.

'I didn't know your mother was going to be there,' she said now, shrinking away from his attempted embrace, and Robert sighed.

'Well of course she's going to be there!' he exclaimed, flinging himself back in his seat. 'As one of the major players in this drama, where else would she be?' His lips twisted. 'Oh, yes, Mama will be present. You don't suppose she's prepared to give Rose any advantage, do you?'

Fliss frowned. 'But I thought—I mean, that night at the Grange, your mother seemed to be trying to make friends——'

'Friends?' Robert snorted. 'Oh, Fliss, sometimes I despair of you, I really do. Do you really think my mother wants to be friends with someone who's halved her income at a stroke?'

Fliss shrugged. 'I don't know.'

'No. That's right. You don't,' said Robert flatly. He gave her a pitying look. 'But you will, soon enough.'

'What do you mean?' Fliss felt anxious. 'Why are you looking at me like that? What's going on?'

Robert dragged his gaze away from her. 'You'll find out,' he said, and then, before Fliss could ask any more questions, he leant forward. 'This is it,' he told the driver. 'You can drop us here.'

Fliss looked about her warily as they got out of the cab. She didn't know what she'd expected when Robert had said they were dining at a club in Chelsea, but she could understand now why he hadn't wanted to bring his own car here. This dingy backwater, with the Thames lapping only a few yards from the end of the alley, was not the salubrious neighbourhood she had imagined. Instead of a doorman and a canopied entrance, there was only a neon sign indicating that the building opposite was indeed a nightclub, and her spirits sank as she anticipated what it must be like inside. What were they doing here? Who could they possibly be going to meet in such sordid surroundings?

'Come on.'

Robert seemed to have no such misgivings, and she had no choice but to follow him across the road, and down the flight of concrete steps that led to the basement entrance.

It crossed her mind as she did so that she was really putting herself in Robert's hands this evening. It was obvious that if she wanted to leave she wasn't going to be able to pick up some passing taxi in this run-down area. Maybe on the Embankment she'd have more luck, but somehow the thought of walking down that alley alone filled her with alarm. No, for her sins, she was compelled to follow her fiancé's lead, and she hoped he had the good sense to keep his wits about him.

They were admitted to the club by a man who could only be described as a bruiser. His scarred and pitted face matched a body as thickly muscled as a boxer's, and his completely bald head was absurdly threatening. Fliss had the feeling she was having some peculiar kind of nightmare, that this couldn't possibly be happening—not to her. But although she pinched herself hard she didn't wake up, and she followed Robert into the club with a fast-beating heart.

Amazingly, once they were through the rather battered door, the atmosphere changed completely. Instead of a smoke-filled room, with worn carpets and grubby tablecloths, Fliss found herself in a brightly lit foyer, where a uniformed hat-check girl took their coats. Robert lifted the velvet cape she had worn to protect herself from the rain from her shoulders, and handed it over, pocketing the ticket with a wry smile.

'Not what you expected, is it?'

Fliss had to concede that it wasn't. 'It's very—nice,' she said lamely, aware of a smell of good food and fine tobacco emanating from the door to the right. Ahead of them, a richly carpeted corridor led away to what appeared to be a casino, and there was muted laughter and low-voiced conversation to calm her fears.

'Nice,' agreed Robert drily. 'Yes, it is, isn't it? Shall we find the others?'

They found Rose Chen in the elegant bar that adjoined the dining-room. She was perched on a high stool, swinging her slim legs; holding court, Fliss thought briefly, and then felt the air leave her lungs as her eyes encountered Oliver's.

He was propped beside Rose, supported by his elbows resting on the bar behind him, but it was the sudden darkening of his expression when he saw her that arrested her breathing. She had thought he would be expecting to see her. After all, this was a *family* occasion, and she was almost family. But the scowl that crossed his face, and the sudden chill that entered his eyes, almost froze her where she stood. He hadn't expected her to be here tonight, that much was obvious. He hadn't wanted her to be here. He was looking at her as if he wished he'd never seen her before, and she longed suddenly for the floor to open up and swallow her.

With an effort she forced herself to look at Rose Chen instead, and saw to her relief that the Chinese woman was too busy introducing Robert to the two other men present to have observed that telling exchange. In a scarlet tunic, slit beyond her knee, and embroidered with dragons, she looked foreign and exotic. No man in his right mind would reject Rose's alien fascination in favour of her own milk-and-water colouring, thought Fliss raggedly. She was almost relieved when Amanda Hastings appeared, and gripped her arm in a painful grasp.

'Well, well, you've certainly made an effort this evening, Fliss,' she remarked, in some surprise. 'Is this all for Robert? Or do you find Mr Lynch as fascinating as I do?'

Fliss tried to sound casual. 'I don't know what you mean.'

'No?' Mrs Hastings looked sceptical. 'Well, no matter. Rose isn't likely to let him go. And you'll be safely out of reach in Hong Kong, while Oliver will be staying here in London.'

Fliss wanted to ask her what she meant by that, but before she could ask her to explain, Robert himself grasped her arm and drew her away. 'My fiancée,' he said, and she realised she was being introduced to the two strangers. 'Fliss, this is——'

'Just call me Tony,' the older of the two men interrupted him easily. 'And this is Vinny,' he added, nodding towards the younger man. 'We're business acquaintances of your fiancé and his family.' He smiled, his rather swarthy features not unattractive in the subdued lighting of the bar. 'It's good to meet you—Fliss, isn't it? I'm pleased to see Jamie's son has his father's good taste.'

'Thank you.'

Fliss smiled and acknowledged the compliment, but she wasn't happy being the centre of attraction. Rose was watching her now, and she could feel Oliver's eyes too, boring into her back.

She accepted a glass of white wine, and then positioned herself well away from the hub of the gathering. Robert had a glass of whisky in his hand, and that seemed to give him all the confidence he needed. Conversation became general, and it wasn't necessary for her to take any part in it. She was quite content to let the others do the talking, listening only desultorily when Robert took the floor.

All the same, she didn't think she liked the way he was attempting to sell himself to the two men, Tony and Vinny. They weren't representative of Hastings' usual clients, she was sure, and she could only assume Rose Chen had invited them to join them. The business acquaintances James Hastings had invited to Sutton Grange—the ones Fliss had met anyway—had been like him: vain, perhaps; pompous, certainly; but basically respectable people. Tony and Vinny weren't like that. They weren't like that at all.

It was strange, because she didn't exactly know what they were like, except that she didn't like them. They were respectably dressed. Their suits were immaculate, their linen whiter than a soap powder commercial. Oliver looked positively sinister beside them. Yet, she'd trust him before she'd trust the others.

'What the—hell—are you doing here?'

Oliver's voice sounded absurdly loud in her ear, and the hesitation before that rather mild epithet was a measure of what he had really wanted to say.

Fliss glanced anxiously at her fiancé, convinced he must have heard Oliver, too, but Robert was too busy ingratiating himself with their guests. He and Rose seemed to be competing for the two men's attention, the Chinese woman's eyes scornful as she watched her half-brother struggling to gain an advantage.

No one appeared to have noticed Oliver's casual removal of himself from one end of the bar to the other. Or if they had, they didn't connect it with Fliss. A quick glance up into his dark face elicited the information that he wasn't even looking at her as he spoke, and Fliss's pulse raced alarmingly as she acknowledged her helpless awareness of his nearness.

'I don't think it's anything to do with you what I do,' she replied at last, in low terse tones. 'And don't worry. I'm not here to tell your girlfriend you've been unfaithful to her!'

It was a calculated risk reminding him of that. By turning the tables on him, she hoped to gain the advantage. If he thought he could intimidate her, he was mistaken. He had just as much to lose as she had. More, in fact, if what Robert said was true.

Oliver swore then, making no concession to her sensitivities this time. 'Believe me,' he said, permitting himself a scathing glance at her shocked face, 'that's the least of my worries.'

Fliss swallowed a mouthful of her wine. 'You don't expect me to believe that.'

'Don't I?' Oliver's mouth curled. 'Trust me, Fliss. I know what I'm talking about.'

Fliss gave him a resentful look. 'I suppose you think she's so infatuated with you, she wouldn't care,' she exclaimed, and Oliver swore again.

'No——'

'Well, I don't believe you. I've seen the way she looks at you. If she knew——'

'Dammit, Fliss, will you quit talking about something of which you know nothing!' Oliver breathed heavily in her ear, and then, calming himself, he went on, 'I don't give a damn what Rose thinks.' He paused, and then continued, 'I should. It's what I'm paid to do, goddamit. But I don't. It's you I care about. Now—do you want to tell me what's going on?'

Fliss stared at him, open-mouthed. 'Oliver——'

'Stop it,' he muttered. 'Stop looking at me like that, and get to the point. I want to know what you're doing here. What did Hastings tell you, for God's sake? Did he inform you who these men are?'

Fliss's throat closed up. 'I—Tony and Vinny,' she said helplessly, trying to instill some strength back into her bones. What had he meant? He *cared* about her? Particularly when he'd just admitted that Rose was supporting him.

'I know their names,' he grated, raising the glass he was holding to his lips. 'I meant, do you know the purpose of this meeting?'

'What do you——?'

'Forget it.' Oliver gave her a warning look. 'Just tell me you've never met them before.'

'But—why?'

'Have you met them before?' His pale eyes narrowed, and she shivered, as much in apprehension at his expression as anything else.

'No,' she conceded at last. 'As far as I know, they're just clients.' She hesitated. 'Rob seems to like them. And—and Rose is practically falling over herself to be polite.'

'Yes.' Oliver finished his drink, and set the empty glass on the bar. 'I noticed.'

Fliss's stomach twisted. 'You're jealous!' she exclaimed, aware as she said the words that, whatever kind of relationship he had with the other woman, she was jealous too.

But Oliver only gave her a pitying look. 'As if,' he said, pushing his hands into his jacket pockets. He looked down at her searchingly for a moment, and then shook his head. 'Nice dress,' he commented mockingly, before walking back to Rose.

# CHAPTER TWELVE

FLISS closed the door of her hotel room behind her and turned the key with trembling fingers. Then, dropping her handbag on to the bed, she walked unsteadily into the bathroom.

She reached the basin just in time. She was sick, violently sick, and even after the awful retching had ceased she could hardly lift her head. Oh, God, she thought, wiping her mouth with shaking fingers. Oh God, what was she going to do? Hastings' weren't just importing antiques, they were importing heroin. Robert's father hadn't made his fortune from selling Chinese porcelain, he'd made it from selling drugs.

She couldn't believe it. She didn't want to believe it. Pushers, dealers, addicts; they were words that belonged to another world. The ruthless men who exploited human suffering for their own gain were gangsters, criminals, villains of low repute. They corrupted people's lives, and were themselves corrupted in the process. But the law was there to deal with them. There was nothing any ordinary citizen could do.

People like her—people who lived decent, honest lives—didn't get involved with such things. They read about them in the morning newspapers, they discussed them over the cornflakes. But they didn't really understand what was actually going on.

God! Fliss drew a trembling breath. It didn't seem possible that people like the Hastingses, who appeared to be so respectable, who lived in the heart of the country and invited the local magistrate to dinner, could participate in such a business.

155

And yet, with hindsight, she could imagine James Hastings enjoying the deception. It must have given him a great deal of pleasure over the years. However dubious his claim to being lord of the manor had been, the fact remained that Sutton Grange had been bought with tainted money. While the villagers had thought he'd been desperate for acceptance, James Hastings must have been laughing at them behind their backs.

And no one had found out. No one had suspected he was anything other than what he seemed. But he had obviously recognised that his son was an unlikely prospect to follow in his footsteps. What a pity Rose Chen hadn't done the same. If she hadn't involved Robert, Robert couldn't have involved her.

Fliss dragged herself up and stared at her reflection in the mirror. God, she looked awful! She doubted even her father would recognise her if he could see her now. She looked so pale and hollow-eyed. She looked like an addict herself.

She sighed. She was fairly sure Robert hadn't intended to be so indiscreet. But, as far as he was concerned, the evening had gone so well that he had drunk more than he could handle.

Rose Chen had realised the danger. Long before Tony and Vinny—was that really their names?—had exhibited any intention of drawing the evening to a close, she had been making it clear that she thought Robert had had enough. Remarks like, 'I think Fliss is getting bored,' or 'Don't you think Fliss looks tired?' were pointed suggestions to take his fiancée back to the hotel. But Robert had been having such a good time, he hadn't wanted to leave.

And he hadn't said anything precisely incriminating in their company, Fliss remembered unwillingly. With Oliver's—as well as Rose's—eyes upon him, he had been careful not to blot his copybook. In any case, she had been so busy coping with her own chaotic feelings, she'd scarcely paid attention to what he had said. But she'd sensed no air of tension as they'd bade them all goodnight.

For herself, she'd been glad to be leaving. The private room, the expertly cooked dinner, the wine which, although she had had little of it, was evidently from a distinctive vineyard, had meant nothing to her. It was the devious game Oliver was playing that had occupied her thoughts. And why, when he'd admitted in so many words that Rose paid his bills, did she care what he did?

Then, on the way home in the chauffeur-driven limousine Tony had lent them, her world had fallen apart. In Robert's boastful ramblings she had heard her father's name disparaged, and when she'd cautioned him about it he'd exposed how he really felt.

It had been disjointed, at first. The resentment Robert felt towards her father mixed up with assertions of the success he was going to make of the business. Matthew Hayton was going to feel pretty sick, he said, when he found out how important Robert really was. *He* wasn't just some poxy country vicar, he added. He had real power.

Of course, Fliss had made excuses for him at first. He had had too much to drink, he was over-excited, and although she'd protested that her father would have nothing but praise if Robert did make a success of his life, she'd consoled herself with the thought he was going to feel pretty sick himself in the morning.

Then Robert's meanderings had taken a different turn. Fumbling in his jacket pocket, he had produced what appeared, in the passing street lights, to be a lacquered snuff box. It was small, and oval-shaped, with a painted lid and a release catch on one side.

Leaning towards her, he had extended the hand holding the snuff box, and tapped his nose conspiratorially. 'Wanna try the merchandise?' he'd asked, with a defiant glance at the chauffeur, and Fliss, who'd assumed

at first it must be a valuable item, had resignedly taken
the box from him.

'Open it,' Robert directed eagerly, his whisky-laden
breath unpleasantly close to her ear, and Fliss obediently pressed the catch.

She didn't know what she had expected might be
inside. Snuff, perhaps; or a precious jewel. Either way,
she wasn't particularly interested when she opened it,
and the sprinkling of white power that spilled onto her
lap as she did so was just an irritation.

It took Robert five seconds to disabuse her of that
notion. His smothered oath, as he snatched the box back
from her, and his added, 'Be careful, can't you?' were
powerful deterrents. She'd never seen a narcotic substance in its purest form before, but she had seen pic-
tures. And the way Robert was glaring at her was
explanation enough.

'Is that——?'

'What do you think?' snapped Robert impatiently, as
the chauffeur glanced curiously over his shoulder. 'One
hundred per cent pure, and you throw it about like con-
fetti! For God's sake, Fliss, this is the breath of life to
some poor bastard!'

Fliss couldn't clearly remember what she'd done next.
The idea that Robert and his family might be involved
in smuggling drugs had seemed too incredible to be true.
She thought she'd looked at him with a little of the horror
she was feeling in her face, and Robert had seemed to
realise—belatedly—that he might have gone too far.

With an impatient shake of his head, he'd slipped the
box back into his pocket, and started talking about
something else. By the time the chauffeur dropped them
at the hotel, she could almost believe she'd imagined the
whole thing.

Almost...

As soon as Robert left her—he needed a nightcap, he
said, and the bar was still open for residents—the

enormity of what had happened had swept over her. Going up to her room in the lift, the nausea that had later become a reality had gripped her. Did he know what he'd done? she wondered. Or was he too full of Scotch to care? Would he remember what had happened in the morning? If she challenged him and he denied it, she had no proof.

She looked down at her skirt suddenly, but the tiny grains of—of what? cocaine? heroin?—had all disappeared. In any case, no one would believe her. Even if she went to the authorities, it was only her word against his.

She shivered suddenly as another thought struck her. If Robert was implicated, Oliver must be implicated, too. It seemed fairly obvious that Rose Chen was at the heart of it. And anyone who lived with her had to know what was going on.

Her breath escaped on a long sigh. Oh, God! Was it only a matter of hours ago that she'd thought the only problem she had was telling Robert she couldn't marry him? How could she tell him now? What was he likely to say? He'd be sure to think it had some bearing on what had occurred this evening. He might not let her go, knowing he had betrayed himself to her.

There was an element of farce to the whole affair, she thought tremulously. But the wild laughter that bubbled in her throat was pure hysteria. Things like this just didn't happen, she told herself unsteadily. Not to women like her, who just wanted a quiet life.

She wished she could blame Oliver. She would have liked to convince herself that this was all his fault. And it was true that until he and Rose Chen came along she had led a fairly placid existence. But it was James Hastings who was the real offender. James Hastings, whose death had set these wheels in motion.

She wondered suddenly how long Robert had known about his father's imperfections. Not long, she suspected, remembering the day of the London meeting, and the strange expression he'd worn when he'd told her he'd been offered a seat on the board. Her father had said that James Hastings had never taken his son seriously. Or perhaps he'd never trusted him to keep his mouth shut.

Whatever, the knowledge that Oliver had made a fool of her, not once but several times, was what hurt the most. As she turned away from the mirror and stumbled back into the bedroom, she wondered why he'd bothered to take the time. Unless—as she'd thought before—it was his way of fooling Robert. It must have given him a great deal of satisfaction to take what Robert had never had...

When someone knocked at the door, Fliss nearly jumped out of her skin. The last thing she had expected was that Robert would trouble her again tonight, and she didn't know if she could even speak to him without betraying how devastated she felt. There was no question of her opening the door. Apart from anything else, she had no desire for anyone to see her in her present state. But tomorrow morning she hoped to have her emotions under control again.

The knock came again, more imperative this time, and she realised she couldn't allow him to wake up the whole floor. This was a respectable hotel, and she had no wish for the management to think that she was anything less than respectable.

She hesitated only a moment, and then went unwillingly nearer. 'Go away, Rob,' she said, in clear, if slightly unsteady tones. 'I'm going to bed.'

'It's not Rob,' a woman responded impatiently and Fliss's lips parted as she recognised Rose Chen's voice. 'I want to talk to you. Open the door.'

Fliss swallowed. 'Um—no——' Her eyes darted desperately around the room, as if looking for a way of escape. 'We've got nothing to say.'

'I disagree.' Rose rattled the handle, and Fliss could imagine how angry she must be to find her way thwarted. 'Open the door, Fliss, unless you want me to cause a scene. I'm quite prepared to say I'm your lover and you won't let me in.'

'You wouldn't!'

Fliss was against the door now, her cheek pressed to the panels, and she distinctly heard Rose's scornful laugh. 'Wouldn't I?' Rose taunted. 'Do you want to take that risk?' Then, 'For pity's sake, open the door. I'm not going to hurt you.'

Fliss straightened. 'What do you want?'

'Let me in and I'll tell you.'

'Robert's not here.'

'I know that.' Rose uttered an impatient sigh. 'You ordered him away, remember? And before you ask, he's not with me.'

'Where is he?'

'Does it matter?' Rose was getting more and more frustrated. 'Drowning his sorrows in the bar, I should imagine. Isn't that usually what he does when he's in trouble?'

'In trouble?'

'Open the door.' Rose was through with trading arguments. 'This is your last chance, Fliss. Any more delay, and I'm going to start shouting.'

Fliss swallowed hard. Then, aware that Rose had her over a barrel, she unlocked the door and opened it. Apart from her own fears, her father would never survive the kind of publicity that would ensue if Rose made good her threat.

Rose was alone. As she stalked into the hotel room, Fliss realised she'd never asked her if she was. For all she knew, Oliver could have been with her.

'Close the door.'

Aware that, for the present, Rose was calling all the shots, Fliss did as she was told. But when she turned around she felt a sudden surge of resentment. This woman wouldn't have caused a scene. She had too much to lose. She'd got in here under false pretences, and Fliss was all kinds of a fool for believing her.

However, Rose's first words prevented the accusation that sprang instantly to her lips. 'You look ghastly!' she sneered scornfully. 'If I didn't know better, I'd say you were desperate for a fix!'

Fliss caught her breath. 'And you'd know, wouldn't you?' she declared recklessly, realising as soon as she'd done so that she'd played right into Rose's hands.

'Would I?' she said, adjusting the fur boa she was wearing across her shoulders. 'Now why would you think that, I wonder? Could it be that my dear brother's been a little indiscreet?'

Fliss took a deep breath and tried to slow her thinking down. No matter how provocative Rose might be, she had to control her panic. She wasn't used to playing this game, whereas Rose knew all the moves.

'I don't know what you mean,' she said now, aware that it was hardly a satisfactory response. 'What do you want? What are you doing here? I'm tired. I'd like to get some sleep.'

'Would you?' Rose regarded her with pitying eyes. Then, tucking the black clutch bag she was carrying beneath her arm, she shrugged her shoulders. 'Well, we don't always get what we want. At least, not in the way that we want it.'

Fliss straightened her spine. 'Is that supposed to mean something?'

'It might.' Rose's lips twisted. 'Don't get clever with me, Fliss. You don't know any of the answers.'

Fliss tried to look confident. 'And you do, I suppose.'

'More than you,' agreed the other woman wryly. 'Though even I don't pretend to know everything.'

'You surprise me.'

Fliss's words were muffled, but Rose heard them, and her eyes glittered dangerously. 'Wait until you hear what I have to say, before you make any more mistakes,' she warned harshly. 'I don't believe you're stupid, and you've got such a lot to lose.'

Fliss pressed her lips together. 'Is that another threat?'

'No. It's the truth,' replied Rose evenly. 'Now—I assume your present appearance is down to your fiancé. And as he's far too drunk to get it—well——' She broke off mockingly. 'Let's just say he hasn't got romance on his mind tonight.'

Fliss coloured. She couldn't help it. It wasn't that what Rose had said had shocked her. It was simply an acknowledgement of her own less than competent state.

'Right.' Rose took her silence for assent, and continued smoothly, 'So we have to suspect that something else has happened to disturb you. And, although I can imagine many things my brother might say which would cause me to want to throw up, you must see him differently. You're going to marry him.'

*Am I?* The words trembled on Fliss's tongue, but this time she had the sense not to say them. She told herself she wasn't scared exactly, but Rose's coming here had unnerved her. If Hastings' were involved in drug smuggling, it would be unwise to make any unwary statements. She'd already made one mistake. She mustn't make a second.

'He did say something, didn't he?' Rose prompted, after a moment, and although Fliss felt safer on her feet, she forced herself to perch on the end of the bed.

'Perhaps,' she conceded at last, realising there was no point in prevaricating. But her knees felt even weaker, now that she was sitting down. She should have remained standing. She doubted she could get up again even if she'd wanted to.

'You don't have to lie to me, Fliss,' Rose exclaimed, and now she offered the other woman a mocking smile.

'Joe—Tony's chauffeur——' she inserted, by way of an explanation '—he heard everything. The idiot showed you the snuff box, didn't he? I warned him to wait until you were married, but Robert never did have any sense. If you'd heard what his father—what *my* father—used to say about him!' She grimaced. 'Oh, well, I suppose it takes all sorts. One day you must tell me what you see in him. I'd really like to know.'

Fliss kept silent with a supreme effort. Rose was clever, she'd give her that. This cosy conversation was not just an attempt to gain her confidence. Mixed in with a kind of homespun tolerance were comments designed to promote a response. If she damned Robert, she damned herself, but if she defended him, would Rose believe her?

'Well?' the Chinese woman demanded at last. 'I'm right, aren't I? Robert did show you the stuff. Do I take it you can't handle it?'

Fliss swallowed. It was hard, harder than she could have imagined to find the right approach. Any casual reaction was obviously faked, but she mustn't behave as if it meant her engagement was over.

'You'll have to give me some time,' she said finally. 'It was a—shock.'

Rose's eyes narrowed. 'I'll bet.'

Fliss waited for her to say something else, but she didn't. And, realising it was up to her to try and convince the woman she wasn't about to go screaming for the police, she added, 'I never suspected, you see. Rob—Rob's father was so—discreet.'

'That's one way of putting it.' Rose hesitated. 'You see now why I want you and—Rob—to go to Hong Kong. He has told you about going to Hong Kong, hasn't he? I think it could be the making of him.'

Or the breaking of him, Fliss thought, with a pang. If it didn't work out, there were ways of dealing with him. Oh, lord, she thought hysterically, was she really thinking that?

'He mentioned it,' she admitted now, hoping Rose wouldn't ask what her response had been. Oh, God, oh, God! What was she going to do?

'Good.' To her relief, Rose seemed to accept her offering, and then, with one of her sudden swings of mood, she said harshly, 'I'm glad you're being so astute. I'd hate to have had to involve your father. From what Oliver tells me, he's a rather sweet old man.'

Fliss's jaw sagged. 'What does my father have to do with anything?' she exclaimed, forgetting for the moment that she had determined not to say anything rash, and Rose regarded her coldly.

'Why—he's our safeguard, of course,' she replied, a long red nail flicking carelessly at her fur coat. 'A—hostage to fortune,' she added without emotion. 'I believe that's the current phrase. I'll have Oliver keep an eye on him. While you're all those miles away.'

# CHAPTER THIRTEEN

'No——' The word slipped out. Fliss couldn't stop it. It was just impossible to imagine marrying Robert now, with or without the prospect of living in Hong Kong. 'That is——' She struggled to control her panic, striving desperately to find the proper words. 'My father isn't involved in this. I don't want him to know.'

'Oh, he won't.' Rose uttered a short laugh. 'At least, not so long as you're a good girl. Robert may be foolhardy, but I assure you I'm not. No, I hear your father likes Oliver. They're becoming quite good friends.'

Fliss felt sick. 'You think so?' she said bitterly, hardly knowing what she was saying in her distress. Was that why Oliver had insinuated himself into their lives? Had his intention only been to neutralise the opposition all along?

'What do you mean?'

Rose's sudden reversion to menace was frightening. Taking a step towards Fliss, she fixed her with an inimical stare, her red mouth thin and threatening.

Fliss licked her lips, unaware at first that she had caused this aggression. 'I don't know what you're talking about,' she said blankly, gripping the edge of the bed with nervous fingers. 'If—if you've said all you came for, I'd really like you to go.'

'I bet you would.' Rose stepped nearer, and to Fliss's dismay, she took a hold of her arm. 'What did you mean when you implied there was some doubt about Oliver's friendship with your father? Is there something more behind it? You'd better tell me, because I mean to find out.'

166

Fliss gulped. 'Let go of me.'

'When I'm ready.' Rose's fingers were amazingly strong, her nails digging into Fliss's flesh. 'Come on, damn you, tell me the truth! What are you hiding?'

'Nothing!' But Fliss was a little scared now. She dreaded to think what Rose would do if she found out that she and Oliver had...

'I don't believe you.' Rose was persistent. Her dark brows descended. 'If I thought your father suspected the truth——'

'Daddy?' Fliss's breath escaped on a strangled laugh. 'You're not serious!' Her relief was such that she was in danger of over-playing her hand. 'I mean—it's not possible. He's a vicar!'

Rose was not convinced. 'You thought Jay-Jay was just an antique dealer,' she reminded her. 'Few of us are what we seem.'

Fliss trembled. 'Who—who is Jay-Jay?'

'Robert's father, of course.' Rose was not diverted. 'So, if your father is just a vicar, why shouldn't I believe Oliver when he tells me your old man is a pushover?'

Fliss's lips tightened. Was that really what Oliver had said? That her father was a pushover? But, perhaps he hadn't been talking about her father at all...

'I haven't said you shouldn't,' she muttered now, seemingly incapable of saying anything that wouldn't evoke an aggressive response. If only Rose would go.

Her nails dug into Fliss's arm suddenly, drawing blood, and she couldn't suppress the cry of protest that escaped her. There was an expression of such malevolence on Rose's face that for a moment she thought she was going to strike her.

But Rose's voice was almost conciliatory when she spoke. 'I know,' she said softly. 'You're afraid I'll find out about your little affair with Oliver.' Her lips were mocking. 'Oh, Fliss, what a lot you've got to learn. I know all about *that*!'

Fliss felt sick. Even though she wouldn't have believed it possible in the circumstances, nausea welled like
a bitter bile in the back of her throat. Oliver had told
her! He had told Rose all about their sordid little
coupling. Oh, God, how could he? And still pretend to
care about her?

But, lost in her misery as she was, she wasn't paying
any attention to Rose's reaction to her silence. For as if
that silence was an admission in itself, the older woman
suddenly issued a hoarse cry. 'I knew it,' she grated. 'I
knew the bastard couldn't keep out of your bed!' And,
with a sudden switch to violence, she brought her hand
back and slapped Fliss full across the face.

'I shouldn't do that again, Rose.'

The hard male voice startled both of them, and Fliss,
her head still ringing from the blow, was hardly relieved
to see someone who at that moment seemed to be the
instigator of all her troubles.

But at least Oliver's appearance caused Rose to release her, even if any reprieve she had had was only likely
to be temporary. With an angry exclamation, the Chinese
woman turned on her erstwhile lover like an enraged
tigress, glaring at him savagely, and spitting out a stream
of invective that happily Fliss couldn't understand.

Oliver, who had been propped against the doorpost,
pushed himself upright, and allowed the door to swing
closed behind him. Fliss didn't know how long he'd been
there, but he seemed unperturbed by Rose's tirade, his
eyes moving briefly over her flushed and dishevelled appearance before returning to the woman before him. He
was a bastard, she thought painfully, covering her
burning cheek with a protective hand. He actually seemed
to be enjoying this.

'That's humanly impossible, Rose,' he remarked
finally, giving some indication of what his girlfriend had
been saying. 'Now, why don't you calm down, and we'll
talk about this like civilised people?'

'Civilised!' Rose fairly choked on the word. 'Don't talk to me about civilised! If it wasn't enough that that fool brother of mine had spilled his guts, now I have to deal with you as well.'

Oliver's eyes narrowed. 'Robert's told someone else?' he asked evenly and Rose gave him a wary look.

'Someone else?' she echoed faintly. 'What are you talking about?'

Oliver took a deep breath and, having successfully diverted her attention from Fliss, pushed his hands into the packets of his trousers. 'Nothing,' he denied carelessly. 'I always thought it was a mistake to trust him, that's all.'

Rose stared at him intently. 'What would you know about it?' she exclaimed. 'You know nothing about antiques.'

'No.' Oliver conceded the point. 'But I know about heroin, and that's what we're really talking about here. Face it, Rose. I wasn't born yesterday.'

The Chinese woman continued to stare at him in silence, but Fliss guessed Rose's brain was working as energetically as her own. Of course, Fliss had assumed Oliver knew what was happening all along. But it didn't make any difference. They were all implicated really— the Hastingses, Rose, Oliver—and the various levels of their involvement didn't mean a thing.

'How did you find out?' Rose asked at last. 'Did Robert tell you?'

'No way.' Oliver regarded her impatiently. 'I was in Vietnam, Rose. I learned to live by my wits. And not knowing who your enemy is is the quickest way to lose your life.'

Rose frowned. 'You think I'm your enemy?'

'No.' Oliver was quick to deny that. 'But your father was. You know he never liked me, Rose. He was always looking for some way to separate us.'

Rose seemed to have forgotten there was anyone else present, and Fliss wished she could just slip out of the door and escape. She didn't want to hear this. She didn't want to know how long Oliver had been Rose's lover, and how he had outwitted her father. She didn't want to hear this. She just wanted to go home, and forget any of this had ever happened.

'You knew about us, before my father died?' Rose was saying now, and although Fliss knew in some curious way that Oliver didn't really want to admit it, he nodded his head. 'You knew about my father?'

'And if I did?'

'Why didn't you tell me?' Rose was sounding less shocked than disbelieving now, though there was no denying her attention was totally focused on the man. 'Lee, if you knew, why didn't you let me know before we came to London. You knew I needed some support. You could have helped me.'

'It's a long story,' said Oliver flatly, and Rose gave him a scornful look.

'It must be,' she agreed, with sudden anger. 'Where did you get your information? And why do I get the feeling I don't want to know?'

Oliver drew a breath. 'I have my sources, Rose. You're not the only one in Hong Kong with a line on what's going down. Think about it, can't you? Do you really believe I can't recognise the signs?'

Rose scowled. 'I'm not a user!'

'No? But I was.' Oliver's mouth curled. 'Come off it, Rose, Hastings knew exactly what he was doing.'

Rose moved her head from side to side. 'I don't believe this.'

'Why?' Oliver appeared to be gaining confidence, and Fliss, who was still reeling from the shock of his confession, closed her eyes against the triumph in his face. 'I think it's time you offered me a piece of the action.

I've certainly got more——' he looked at Fliss, and amended his words '—guts—than your brother.'

What happened then seemed afterwards to happen in slow motion. Fliss saw Oliver pull his hands out of his pockets, and Rose, who must have believed he was carrying a gun, groped awkwardly for her bag. It was ludicrous really, because all Oliver did was spread his hands towards her, but the bullet that caught him in the chest was all too unhappily real.

'Bitch!' he said chokingly, falling back against a chair, and then the door was flung open behind him, and three other men with automatics burst into the room...

Fliss's father collected her from the hospital the following morning. The authorities had wanted to contact him the night before, but she had insisted on them waiting until it was light. She was all right, after all. They had only kept her in the hospital overnight for observation. She was tired, and a little shaky, but not injured. Well, not in body anyway, she amended. Her mind—her psyche—was something else.

Matthew Hayton didn't say anything until they had cleared the city centre, concentrating on his driving, and giving his daughter time to marshall her thoughts. He was more concerned with her white face than with any physical pain she might have suffered. He had the feeling it would take her more than twenty-four hours to recover from the shock.

But, when they were safely on the M40 heading westward, he felt compelled to say something, *anything*, to bring some life back into her pale features. However loath she was to discuss what had happened, she really ought to talk about it. Bottling it up was not going to help, and not everyone would be as understanding as himself.

She'd already been told that the police would want to speak to her again within the next couple of days. She had made a preliminary statement, but there was more, much more, that they would have to discuss with her. Not least, how much she had known about her fiancé's business; and why she hadn't called the police as soon as she'd learned the truth.

'Tough night,' commented Matthew Hayton softly, and Fliss turned a strained face in his direction.

'Mmm,' she murmured, finding it difficult to speak at all without breaking down. 'Um—thanks for coming to get me. You don't know how good it is to—to——'

'I can imagine,' her father interrupted her gently. 'I'm just sorry I didn't see this coming. It's not as if I haven't heard gossip about Hastings in the past. But a man in my profession is only supposed to see the good in people. And casting doubts on a man's character does seem a rather un-Christian thing to do.'

'Oh, Daddy!'

'Well.' He sighed. 'It's over now. From what the officer told me, I gather both Robert and his mother have been arrested. They'd apparently been suspicious of their operation of some time. The arrival of the daughter only accelerated the proceedings.'

'Yes.' Fliss didn't really want to discuss it. The success of the police operation, and her own rescue at their hands, meant nothing. All she could see was Oliver's face when Rose Chen fired her gun.

'It was a shame anyone had to be injured,' went on Matthew Hayton ruefully. 'Although I suppose Lynch was as guilty as the rest.' He paused. 'Whatever you say, I know you liked him, Felicity. But you could never have had a life with a man like him.'

'Do you mind if we don't talk about it?' Fliss stared blindly through the car's window, trying to make some sense of her mixed emotions. She hadn't cared about Oliver Lynch, she'd despised him. So why did she mourn him now that he was dead?

'If you insist.' Matthew Hayton gave her a sideways glance. 'But you're going to have to talk about it soon, darling. I'm sorry, but it won't just go away.'

Fliss bent her head. 'I know.'

Her father hesitated. 'That bruise, on your cheek—did Lynch do that?'

'No!' Fliss lifted her hand and laid her palm along her jawline. 'I—it was Rose—Rose Chen.' She licked her lips, and then added in a muffled voice, 'Oliver prevented her from hitting me again, actually. If—if he hadn't followed her back to the hotel, who knows what might have happened.' She sniffed, and then murmured barely audibly, 'Who knows? He might have got away.'

'And you'd have been glad if he had?' her father suggested, proving his hearing was still as sharp as ever, and Fliss gave him a defensive look.

'Perhaps.'

'In other words, you were attracted to him,' Matthew Hayton declared forcefully. 'Oh, Felicity, the man was a criminal!'

'So was—*is*—Robert,' she retorted painfully, and her father shook his head.

'Even so...'

Fliss stifled a sob. 'Well, it doesn't matter anyway, does it?' she asked him unsteadily. 'As you've just said, it's over. At least you won't have to worry about me ever seeing him again.'

# CHAPTER FOURTEEN

'I'M LEAVING now, Felicity. Are you sure you don't want to change your mind and come, too?'

'Quite sure, thanks.'

Fliss looked up at her father and endeavoured to appear apologetic and nothing else. It wouldn't do for him to think she was still depressed. In the last two weeks, since she had learned there was to be an epilogue to her relationship with Oliver, she had made a concerted effort to assuage her grief.

'Well, if that's your final word...' Matthew Hayton regarded his daughter with a disturbingly shrewd gaze. Whatever she thought, he knew she was still suffering. And there was something she wasn't telling him, of that he had no doubt.

'It's so cosy here,' exclaimed Fliss, from the comfortable depths of her father's armchair. She spread the skirt of her navy pinafore dress over her legs, and smiled appealingly. He couldn't know that the book in her hand was unread. The picture she presented was surely convincing enough. 'It's raining,' she added. 'You go and enjoy the play. You can tell me all about it when you get back.'

Her father looked as if he might object but, then, with a resigned shake of his head, he buttoned his overcoat. 'I suppose it isn't the most exciting prospect,' he agreed. 'Amateur dramatics aren't really my line either, and the church hall isn't the warmest place on a chilly autumn evening.'

'I'm sure you'll enjoy it,' Fliss assured him firmly, and he pulled a wry face.

'I just don't like leaving you alone, that's all.' He shook his head, and then went on reluctantly, 'Whatever you say, I know you're still fretting over—over that man, Oliver Lynch.'

'Oh, Dad!'

'I know I'm right.' Matthew Hayton gave in to the urge to seek her confidence yet again. 'Ever since the authorities decided you couldn't help them any more, you've refused to talk about what happened, about *him*. I'm sure it would be better if you——'

'Not now, Dad.' Fliss spread the folds of her skirt over her knees, realising she would have to talk to her father sooner or later. 'Um—you're going to be late——'

'Do you think I care?' Her father gazed at her worriedly. 'You're not deceiving me, you know, Felicity. Was he really worth all this soul-searching?'

Fliss sighed. 'No,' she admitted, after a moment. She concentrated on the glowing embers burning in the grate. 'No, I don't suppose he was. But give me time, Dad. It is only three months.'

'Three months.' Matthew Hayton raised his eyes heavenward. 'It seems like three years!'

'Oh, Daddy.' Fliss looked at her father for a moment, and then unfolding her legs, she got to her feet. 'I love you,' she said, going to kiss his cheek. 'And we will talk, I promise. Maybe tomorrow, hmm?'

'Tomorrow,' he agreed warmly, hugging her in return. 'I won't let you forget.'

'OK.' She accompanied him to the door. 'Now—enjoy your evening. I intend to enjoy mine.'

But after her father had gone Fliss trudged back into the living-room on rather heavier feet. It wasn't easy trying to behave as if it was only a matter of time before she snapped out of her misery. The way she felt at the moment, it was hard to believe she'd ever get over it.

To begin with, she had had a lot to occupy her. The police investigation, the interviews, the questions; they might not have helped to ease her pain, but they had given her something else to think about. But that was all over now. The court case was still pending, of course, but it didn't look as if her evidence was going to be needed. Robert had broken down during his interrogation, and his evidence had gone a long way in implicating his mother. They were both in custody now, the house was closed up, and the twins, whom Fliss had felt sorry for, had been despatched to distant relatives in Scotland.

Of course, she knew Rose Chen had been arrested too, but in her case the charges would include murder. Oliver's murder, she thought, with the agonising ache she always felt when she thought of him. Whatever else Rose was convicted of, his death would always be on her conscience.

The urge to weep swept over her, but she forced herself not to give in to her tears. Tears wouldn't help her. They wouldn't help the tiny pulse of life that lived inside her. Her father was right. They had to talk. He might not be able to forgive her when he knew.

Looking down, she shaped the curve of her stomach with searching hands. As yet there was little to see. Certainly nothing was visible through her clothes. But when she was naked, when she stood in front of her dressing-table mirror and studied her body, it was a different story. The solid little mound of her pregnancy was unmistakable.

Dropping her hands, she moved back to the chair and picked up her book. It was just as well her father was used to seeing her in loose shirts and dresses. As yet he'd made no point of the fact that she'd stopped wearing trousers. But it was nearly four months now. She would have to tell him soon.

She sat down, and the book dropped unheeded from her fingers. A baby, she thought, still with a certain amount of incredulity. Oliver's baby. He never would have the chance to learn that he was going to become a father. Would it have made a difference? Would he have asked her to wait for him until he was free?

More to the point, would she have done it? she wondered unhappily. But it was only a fleeting thought. She knew that if Oliver had asked her, she'd have followed him to the ends of the earth.

It was ironic really. When Robert had asked her to go with him to Hong Kong she'd instinctively fought against it. Yet she knew she'd have lived anywhere with Oliver. With him, she'd learned what loving someone could mean.

Did that make her a bad person? she wondered. How would her father feel when he learned what she had done? Nothing could alter the fact that she had betrayed her promises. And he was going to have to face his parishioners in the face of her disgrace.

Of course, everyone would think it was Robert's baby, and that was something else she was going to have to deal with. There was no way she was going to let her child grow up not knowing who his real father was. Oliver's death might not have been an heroic one, but he had been protecting her.

The sound of a car drawing up outside brought a look of anxiety to her face. Obviously someone didn't know her father was attending the amateur dramatic society's production at the church hall this evening. And, as Reverend Matthew Hayton's services were rarely needed in the evenings except in emergencies, she got up at the first ring of the bell.

She had turned on the hall light, so that when she opened the door the man sheltering in the porch outside was immediately visible. His dark hair flecked with raindrops, his collar turned up against the weather, he stood waiting patiently for her to recognise him.

And she did. Oliver's features, though gaunt, were instantly identifiable, and a wave of dizziness swept over her. The rain was driving down beyond the roof of the porch, and although she cast a panic-stricken look up and down the street there was no sign of another living soul.

But Oliver wasn't living, she reminded herself unsteadily. He was dead, and whoever it was standing here on her porch it was not Oliver. She was either blind or hallucinating, and she clutched the doorpost weakly in an effort to control her fears.

'Hello, Fliss.'

The voice was the same. It was Oliver's voice, Oliver's lips that twitched in sudden ruefulness, Oliver's hand that reached to cover hers where it rested on the wood.

'Don't.'

Fliss pulled her hand away before he could touch her, pressing both hands together over the slight rise of her stomach, as if in protection of her unborn child. She wasn't sure, but she didn't think she'd ever fainted before, yet she knew she was near to it now. Standing here, staring at a dead man's face, she felt the first flicker of darkness nudging at her temples.

'It's me, Fliss.' Oliver took her obvious withdrawal for repugnance, but he didn't disappear as she'd hoped, or show any signs of going away. 'I know it's late, but I didn't get in from the States until a couple of hours ago. This weather isn't confined to England, and the flight was delayed——'

'Go away!'

Unable to stand it any longer, Fliss tried to close the door against him, but somehow his foot was in the way, and she fled on panicky feet back into the living-room. She half expected to see herself, as you did in nightmares, fast asleep by the fire, but her chair was empty.

And footsteps were coming along the hall, undeterred by her attempt to thwart him.

'Fliss,' he exclaimed wearily, appearing in the doorway like some malevolent ghost. 'For God's sake, Fliss, will you listen to me? It's really me. I'm alive. The news of my death was faked!'

Fliss came round to find herself lying comfortably on the couch. For a moment the awareness of where she was confused her. Hadn't she been sitting in her father's chair? She frowned. She must have moved because she was tired. She certainly felt a little shaky at the moment.

She blinked, and as she did so, she caught sight of a tall, dark figure standing on the hearth. It was a man, but it wasn't her father. And suddenly the whole terrifying scenario swept over her again.

At once, she struggled to sit up, but Oliver's tired voice arrested her. 'Relax,' he said heavily. 'I'm not going to touch you. I'm sorry if I frightened you earlier, but it wasn't meant to be that way.'

Fliss ignored his instructions, and pushed herself up against the cushions. 'You're not dead,' she ventured unsteadily, still not prepared to believe the evidence of her own eyes, and Oliver sighed.

'Not nearly,' he agreed flatly. 'The reports were, as they say, an exaggeration.'

Fliss stared at him. 'But—the police said——'

'I know what the police said,' Oliver interrupted her wearily. 'They said what they were told to say. It suited everyone's purpose if I was assumed to be deceased.'

Fliss swallowed. 'Whose purpose? Aren't you—aren't you wanted for—for questioning?'

'Oh, I've been questioned,' Oliver assured her drily. Then, glancing round, 'Can I sit down? I guess you deserve an explanation. Though it's just possible you may not like it.'

'You mean you turned informer,' Fliss exclaimed, capable of no other interpretation for his being here, and Oliver sighed.

'In a manner of speaking,' he said, making little effort to defend himself. 'I certainly told them what I knew. It was fairly futile as it happens. Hastings condemned them all as soon as he opened his mouth.'

Fliss shook her head. 'But why are you here? Why aren't you——?'

She broke off, and Oliver gave her a rueful look. 'In prison, like the rest of them?' he suggested drily, and she nodded.

'Well—you were involved, weren't you? I mean—you told Rose you knew what was going on.'

Oliver glanced behind him, and then lowered his weight into her father's chair. In the light from the fire behind him, Fliss could see the lines of strain that bracketed his mouth. Whatever had happened to him, it hadn't been as easy as she thought.

'I guess it looked that way, didn't it?' he said now. 'But appearances aren't always what they seem.'

Fliss's hands trembled. 'But you were with Rose. You were—*her*—lover.'

Oliver spread his legs, and linked his hands together in the space between. 'I slept with her,' he amended evenly. 'Until I met you, it was no problem.' Then, as Fliss's stomach quivered he added carelessly, 'But you have to know I didn't *love* her. When we were together, love simply didn't come into it.'

Fliss pressed her shoulders back against the cushions. 'Is that supposed to be an explanation? Do you really expect me to believe you weren't part of that whole drug scene?' She caught her breath. 'For God's sake, Oliver, I was there, remember? Don't expect me to forget the things you said.'

Oliver shrugged. 'I gave up expecting anything a long time ago, Fliss,' he said flatly. 'But, for what it's worth,

I never was involved. I was working for the United States government. I was recruited in Hong Kong many years ago.'

Fliss gasped. 'You're not serious!'

'Funny.' Oliver gave her a telling look. 'I thought I was.'

Fliss swung her feet to the floor and sat up. 'It's not possible.'

'I'm here.'

'Yes, but——' She sought for an explanation. 'You said yourself that you'd been an informer.'

'I said in a manner of speaking,' corrected Oliver, regarding her with weary, hooded eyes. 'I know it wasn't a pleasant job I was doing. But if you'd seen the victims of the trade, you might have more compassion.'

Fliss moistened her lips. 'So——' She couldn't get the words out at first, and she had to try again. 'I—why didn't you——?' She had been going to say, 'let me know', but she realised that was too presumptuous and changed it to, 'let anyone know?'

'As I said before, it was easier if I was believed dead.'

'But why?'

'Fliss, we're not dealing with choirboys here. These men are dangerous. I doubt my life would have been worth a plugged nickel in the days before Robert confessed. And even then——'

'So you—went back to the United States?' Fliss was trying to make sense of what he was saying, and Oliver gave her a wry smile.

'Not initially, no.' He paused. 'I had a bullet wound to contend with. The doctors wouldn't let me travel, until I was out of Intensive Care.'

Fliss gulped. 'You really were shot, then?'

'I really was shot,' he agreed drily. 'I'll show you the scar some time. They patched me up real good.'

Fliss pressed a hand to her stomach. 'I can't take this in.'

'No.' Oliver looked sympathetic. 'Well, I guess it is a lot to handle right away.' He paused. 'Do you want me to come back tomorrow? I wanted to speak to your father, but I see he doesn't appear to be around.'

'He's—he's at a play. In the church hall,' said Fliss quickly, feeling a hollowing in her stomach at the realisation that Oliver must have come here to see her father and not her. 'He won't be back for a couple of hours.' She hesitated. 'Are—are you staying in the village?'

'I just got off Concorde,' Oliver reminded her quietly, pressing down on the arms of the chair, and getting to his feet. 'I may just drive back to London. I don't feel like being sociable this evening.'

Fliss got up, too, and for a moment there was only a hair's breadth between them. But then, as if unwilling to give her the wrong impression a second time, Oliver moved away, running a hand through his rain-splashed hair, and heading unmistakably for the door.

'Um—you could stay here,' Fliss found herself saying hurriedly, and Oliver turned to give her a wary look. 'Well, we do have plenty of room,' she defended herself quickly. 'And—and I'm sure my father would like to see you.'

'But not you, hmm?' Oliver murmured softly, and she stared at him disbelievingly as his gaze sought hers.

'I—didn't say that,' she protested, shaking her head. 'I—of course I'm pleased to see you. I—I thought you were dead, for heaven's sake! Finding out you're not, I—I just don't know what to say.'

'Can you forgive me?'

'Forgive you?' Fliss's mind spun wildly in all directions, trying to ascertain what he was meaning. 'Oh—you mean for what happened between us? Well—I suppose that was as much my—my fault as yours.'

'That's not what I mean.' Oliver turned fully to face her. 'I meant for deceiving you; for being involved in your fiancé's arrest and eventual conviction. Dammit, Fliss, I'm sorry. I didn't mean for you to get hurt.'

Fliss trembled. 'Robert—Robert and me—that was over before—before I found out about—about——'

'About what was going on?'

'Yes.'

Oliver stared at her. 'Why?'

'Why?' Fliss caught her lower lip between her teeth, wishing she knew how to answer him. 'Well—I suppose because I realised I didn't love him. He—he asked me to go to Hong Kong, and that's when I knew it was over.'

Oliver took a step towards her. 'You mean you'd changed your mind before he was arrested?'

'Yes.' Fliss cleared her throat. 'My father guessed before I did. He—he thought it was because of you.'

Oliver caught his breath. 'And was it?'

Fliss bent her head. 'I didn't want to think so.'

'But was it?' Oliver's voice was taut.

'Does it matter?'

'God, of course it matters.' With a smothered oath, he covered the last few feet that separated them, and took hold of her shoulders. 'Are you saying that my making love to you meant something to you? If it meant half as much to you as it did to me, I might believe I stand a chance.'

Fliss looked up at him. 'Oh, Oliver...'

'Tell me,' he exhorted her fiercely. 'Come on, Fliss. I need to know.'

Fliss pressed her lips together for a moment. 'Yes,' she said simply, incapable of denying him. 'But you didn't come back to hear that, did you? You came back to see my father.'

'Don't talk——'

The rest of what he said was muffled against her lips, and Fliss was in no state to demand an answer. Besides, she had her answer in the welcome possession of his hands, and the hungry affirmation of his mouth.

He kissed her many times, long, drugging kisses that took her breath and bruised her lips. His tongue invaded her mouth, seeking its own fulfilment, and she clutched his neck eagerly, half afraid even now that she was dreaming.

But when his hands moved down her body, drawing her closer, making her instantly aware of the pulsing heat of his arousal, Fliss was forced to resist him. Much as she wanted to give in, to yield to him, to feel again the hard strength of him inside her, there was still so much that hadn't been said, so much she had to know.

And Oliver, sensing her withdrawal, allowed her to put an inch of space between them. 'I know,' he said, resting his forehead against hers. 'I'm not going to rush you this time. Don't worry, love. We have all the time in the world.'

Fliss took a trembling breath. 'Yes, but——'

'And I know your father's quite likely to come back soon,' he added, 'particularly if someone happens to tell him there's an unfamiliar car at your gate. Relax, sweetheart. I don't expect you to climb into bed with me—at least——' his lips twisted '—not yet, at any rate. I realise I still have some explaining to do, so why don't we sit right down and do it?'

'Do what?'

'Talk,' he said, giving her an old-fashioned look. 'Don't tease me, Fliss. It's not easy behaving like a sane and sensible guy. These last three months have been hell, believe me.'

And for me, thought Fliss ruefully, but she didn't say it. For the moment, it was enough just to try and absorb the fact that Oliver wasn't dead, that he cared about her, that her baby might have a father after all.

But, for a while after Oliver had shed his jacket and they had settled on the sofa, there was an intimate silence in the room, punctuated only by little sighs and murmurs, and the satisfying melding of mouths and tongues. It was difficult to be sensible when they had so much time to make up, but after Oliver had taken her hand and pressed it to the throbbing hardness of his body Fliss at least knew something must be said.

'Tell me about what happened,' she murmured, ducking out of any explanations she had to make, and with a brief closing of his eyes, and a final arching of his hips against her, Oliver gave in.

'You know most of it already,' he said, settling her head on his shoulder, and resting his head back against the cushions. 'I was supposed to keep close to Rose, to find out how the merchandise was being distributed in England. We knew some of it was finding its way to the States via London, and my boss was hoping Rose would make me her confidant.'

Fliss bit her lip. 'And did she?'

'Not really. Rose was too wary for that. Her only mistake was involving Robert. James Hastings had recognised his son's weaknesses early on.' He shrugged. 'But I was able to keep my boss informed of her movements, even if the computer disk I copied and sent him turned out to be no use.'

'Go on.'

'What I didn't know was that the British authorities were working alongside us. That was something Archie chose not to tell me, obviously in case I made any mistakes. But that meeting at the club was exactly what they wanted. Only, when they moved in, our mutual friend had gone.'

'Rose?'

'Yeah, Rose.'

'So—when she came to the hotel——'

'God knows what she intended. Of course, she didn't know the police were involved, though I know she was suspicious of me.'

'Why?'

Oliver hesitated. 'It was a job, Fliss. And it was no real hardship to begin with. Rose is a beautiful woman, and I'd be lying if I said I objected to the assignment in the beginning. But—after I met you my relationship with Rose became an anathema to me. It was all I could do to speak to her, let alone anything else.'

'But you did go on—going to bed with her, didn't you?'

'Would you believe me if I said no?'

'I don't know.' Fliss lifted her shoulders. 'Try me.'

Oliver sighed. 'Rose and I weren't living together. Not in Hong Kong or London. We each had our own place. I admit, things were different in Hong Kong. But after we came to London she was too wrapped up in the business to feel any sense of neglect.' He grimaced. 'Actually, she thought she was neglecting me.' He paused. 'Except when she saw us together.'

'Is that true?'

He held up one hand. 'I swear.'

Fliss snuggled closer. 'That night—the night you were shot—did you know the police were following you?'

'Hell, no. All I was concerned about was you.' He shook his head. 'I knew I had to do something to stop Rose from hurting you, but when she pulled out that gun I thought I'd had it.'

'I thought you had, too,' murmured Fliss, in a muffled voice, remembering the horror she had felt when Oliver had slumped, bleeding, to the floor. The arrival of the men who had rescued her and arrested Rose had meant little compared to the anguish she had felt when she'd thought Oliver was dead. She'd wanted to die as well.

'Well, as you can see, I didn't,' Oliver murmured now, nuzzling her cheek. 'They whipped me off to a safe hospital, and I spent the next four weeks recovering from my injuries. They wouldn't let me see anyone or talk to anyone. Even my own parents were kept in the dark.

Then Archie had me shipped out to Hong Kong, and I flew to the States from there.'

Fliss frowned. 'Who is Archie?'

'Colonel Archibald Lightfoot. He was my controller. It was he who insisted on complete confidentiality, until he had Rose safely back in Hong Kong.'

'I see. But Rose can't be charged with your murder now.' She paused. 'Does she know you're not dead?'

'She does now.' Oliver grimaced. 'She wasn't very happy about it. But then, Rose never was a good loser.'

'But won't she——?'

'Fliss, Fliss. What they have on Rose will put her away until she's a very old lady. She had used that gun before, you know. She wasn't an amateur.'

Fliss shivered. 'You're not still going to work in Hong Kong, are you?' she ventured, and to her relief Oliver shook his head.

'That was another reason why I wanted to visit the States before I came here. I wanted to know if I had a job to go back to. My father—he's a judge, by the way,' he added modestly, 'thinks he may be able to put in a good word for me.'

'I see.' Fliss licked her lips. 'And that's important to you?'

'More important than you, you mean?' Oliver suggested, guessing immediately what she meant. 'No, my love, no one's more important than you. But until I got here, until I looked at you and saw that you could forgive me, I honestly didn't know if I stood a chance.'

'Well, you do,' mumbled Fliss, burrowing against him. 'Oh, Oliver, I'm so glad you came back. I—there's something you don't know, you see. Something I have to tell you. I just hope you'll understand. I'm not very good at making confessions.'

Oliver frowned now, and because he was looking so intently at her, Fliss felt obliged to straighten up. 'It's— it's just—this,' she said awkwardly, and grasping his hand, she laid it on the swelling mound that marked her waistline.

Oliver's eyes darkened. 'You're pregnant!'

'Mmm.' Fliss swallowed. 'I'm sorry.'

'You're *sorry*?' Oliver scowled. 'Isn't it mine?'

Fliss gazed at him with indignant eyes. 'I—I——' she spluttered. 'Of course, it's yours. I don't. I haven't——'

'I know.' Oliver pulled her eagerly back into his arms. 'But when you said you were sorry——' He groaned. 'God, don't be sorry about our baby.' He gave a short laugh, but she could tell he was almost as stunned by the news as she had been by his appearance. 'I'm going to be a father! I can't believe it! Wait until my parents hear about this!'

Fliss gazed up at him. 'You don't mind, then?'

'Mind?' He gulped. 'My love, I'm delighted. You're going to have to marry me now. I won't take no for an answer.'

Their son was born five months later. Benjamin Lynch came into the world without too much effort on his mother's part, and Oliver, who had stayed with Fliss throughout the long night preceding the birth, was there to hand the baby to his wife.

'He's like you,' said Fliss, at once, studying the baby's dark features with a marvellous feeling of well-being. 'Can you see? He's got your nose.' She smiled. 'I wonder what he's thinking now.'

'He's wondering who that beautiful creature is who's making such a fuss of him,' declared Oliver drily, unable to resist brushing her damp hair back from her forehead. 'How do you feel? Are you tired?'

Fliss smiled up at him. 'Do I look tired?'

'You look gorgeous,' Oliver averred, wedging his hips on to the bed beside her. 'But we won't do this too often, hmm? I don't think I can stand the strain.'

'Silly.' Fliss stroked her husband's rough cheek with a caressing finger. 'It was easy. I could do it all again.'

'Well, I couldn't,' said Oliver. 'And I'd like my wife to myself for a while. As soon as junior's old enough, we're going to have that honeymoon I promised you.'

'We had a honeymoon.'

'I mean, when there's just the two of us,' replied Oliver wryly. 'With nothing to come between us. Not even Ben.'

'Ben.' Fliss smiled again. 'Benjamin Matthew Lynch. I like it.'

'I'm sure your father will like it, too,' said Oliver, bending to kiss her cheek. 'He always says he knew what was going on before we did.' He shook his head. 'Oh, baby, do you know how much I love you? I'm never going to let you go.'

'That's good.' Fliss reached up to kiss him. 'Because you know what? I feel exactly the same.'

# HARLEQUIN®

## PRESENTS
## RELUCTANT BRIDEGROOMS

Two beautiful brides, two unforgettable romances...
two men running for their lives....

*My Lady Love,* by Paula Marshall, introduces
Charles, Viscount Halstead, who lost his memory
and found himself employed as a stableboy by the
untouchable Nell Tallboys, Countess Malplaquet.
But Nell didn't consider Charles untouchable—
not at all!

*Darling Amazon,* by Sylvia Andrew, is the story of
a spurious engagement between Julia Marchant
and Hugo, marquess of Rostherne—an engagement
that gets out of hand and just may lead Hugo to
the altar after all!

Enjoy two madcap Regency weddings this May,
wherever Harlequin books are sold.

If you are looking for more titles by

**ANNE MATHER**

Don't miss these fabulous stories by one of Harlequin's most distinguished authors: